The Mattress

Sophie Frank was born in Manchester in 1961. One of her short stories, 'Birth', was published in Heinemann's *Best Short Story Collection 1988*. Since then her work has appeared in the British journals *Ambit* and *The Fred*, the Australian *Overland Extra* and *Scarp*, and in *First Fictions: Introduction 11*, published by Faber and Faber in 1992. Over the last ten years she has lived in both Sydney and London. *The Mattress Actress* is her first novel.

THE
MATTRESS ACTRESS

Sophie Frank

faber and faber
LONDON BOSTON

First published in 1993
by Faber and Faber Limited
3 Queen Square London WC1N 3AU

Typeset by Intype, London

Printed in Great Britain by
Clays Ltd, St Ives Plc

All rights reserved

© Sophie Frank, 1993

Sophie Frank is hereby identified as author of this work
in accordance with Section 77 of the Copyright,
Designs and Patents Act 1988

*This book is sold subject to the condition that it shall not, by way of trade
or otherwise, be lent, resold, hired out or otherwise circulated without the
publisher's prior consent in any form of binding or cover other than that
in which it is published and without a similar condition including
this condition being imposed on the subsequent purchaser.*

A CIP record for this book is
available from the British Library

ISBN 0–571–16952–X

2 4 6 8 10 9 7 5 3 1

For Hassan Bayouni

'To their class I owe a debt of gratitude; they have been my refuge in sorrow, an unfailing relief in my miseries, have saved me from drinking, gambling or perhaps worse . . . They are what society has made them and society uses them, enjoys them, even loves them; yet denies them, spurns them, damns and crushes them even whilst frequenting and enjoying them. In short it shamefully ill-treats them in most Christian countries and more so in Protestant England than in any others that I know.'

'Walter', *My Secret Life* (1880)

'Although prostitution is considered to be a uniquely human profession, there is some evidence to the contrary from both field and laboratory studies of non-human primates. Chimpanzees have been observed in the wild engaging in sexual activity in exchange for food, and in a laboratory study in which tokens were given to chimps for specific behaviours, observers suddenly noticed that a few female chimps had all the tokens. Further observation revealed a form of prostitution.'

Priscilla Alexander, *Prostitution: A Difficult Issue for Feminists*
(Bullough, 1978)

PART ONE

Let me introduce myself. I live in Sydney, Australia, and my name is Ruby Hart. I wasn't born with a name like that but I never felt the name Julie was me. It's a thin name, slipping and sliding and melting and spreading like warm margarine on a hot knife blade. It's the kind of name little girls are given alongside frilly dresses, white knee-socks and black shiny shoes. Ruby Hart.

I changed my name when I met John, which is when I began working. I use the name Ruby at home and at work, which is odd, given the divisions I make between one and the other.

Throughout all of this I don't ask anything but that you do not judge. Open your ears like barn doors and leave them open. Be very quiet, be very still and listen. For I have my story. This is what it's about: how to keep what you are born with. How to go back. How to blush like a child. How to step outside the circle game and march straight, best foot forward, upright, chin out, chest out, on and on and on and on like a clockwork tin soldier.

My husband is a mad man. No, I didn't say good – which also ends in 'd'; I said mad. Crazy. Doolally. One short of a load. Not good or bad, no worse than the rest, but mad. 'He's got one crack too many in his plasterwork, Ruby,' someone once said. My hackles rose. I would defend John. 'We don't exactly live on the San Bernardino fault.' Right up to the end I would defend, if not him, at least our relationship.

'Just look at his eyes,' someone else would say. I didn't want to hear. I loved those eyes – their imperfections, their sand-grain flecks, their size, their skew-wiffness, the way one collected the change while the other strolled home from the shop. I sang songs to those eyes. 'Look at what about his eyes?' I'd retort, suddenly getting angry. 'There are too many pink threads running through the white of them . . . It's not healthy. They look like a map of the Nile delta.'

Nor is John's laugh healthy. He stores it all up and then sets it free in one big cloud burst. His face curls up and he's off with a high falsetto laugh which won't stop.

Tonight had been bad, but no worse than other nights. If anything, in fact, it had been better in that this time I had escaped bruise-free and scot-free. I had managed to dart into the bathroom and lock the door behind me.

When the door was firmly closed and I was safe, I hadn't sat down on the warm wooden loo seat brooding over the decision, chewing it over as I normally would have done. It just happened. It was something that I had known would happen, at some time, according to its own rhythm. Once it did I sat back, watched and enjoyed.

When the thuds had been over for ten minutes or so and I could hear the vroom-vroom, like a purring car engine, of his snores, I tiptoed out, grabbed a few things from the wardrobe, stuffed them into the nearest container – a polythene bag – and left.

The purple-and-white-striped taxi glides through the empty night-time roads. Being a cab driver must be like being a whore: people come into your space who you don't want to see but who you are inviting to pay the bills. One drunk is the same as the next. These days taxis have bullet-proof glass. Like condoms, the glass protects. It separates us from them.

Sydney is beautiful at night with the twinkly tiara lights of the harbour, but though we're going right beside the water, down by Rose Bay, I don't look out of the windows as I usually would. Instead I focus on the swaying crucifix which dangles from the driver's rear-view mirror and then I count the wooden bobbles of his seat cover. They come in rows of fifty.

As I'm counting them, I feel nothing. I feel completely numb.

I'm an actress in my own life. I'm watching it at the movies. I'm absent. I have gone away; I have abandoned myself.

'Where to, luv?'

The taxi pulls into the glaring neon lights of the tunnel and comes out on William Street. Although it's near four in the morning, the transsexuals are still out, unstoppable on amphetamines, dancing round the lampposts in their glittery, spangly clothes. A steady stream of kerb-crawlers stop-starts past them, most of the fuckwit jerks looking for kicks not tricks.

Sometimes I feel scarred. Sometimes I feel tainted. I burst out at ordinary facts of life – for example, the kerb-crawlers. Calm it, Ruby. I'm even talking to myself now. Ruby, calm down. Fast-forward the years and I could become a bag lady, a rattling old crone on a street corner with a supermarket trolley full of old newspapers serving as a mobile home.

'Turn left . . . Up there, up Bourke.'

The cabbie, out to impress, twists a hard left and swerves up Bourke Street. We pull up outside a shabby block of fifties flats. This is sanctuary.

Foreseeing the future, two or three months ago Anita had given me keys to her flat. We were walking along the front at Bondi at the time, strutting our stuff on the patch of concrete before the Pavilion, and her gift came as a surprise. Why would I need them? 'You just might,' she had replied, and had added, under her breath, 'When you get your head together.' I was insulted but I said nothing.

She comes off the air at three, so when I arrive the flat is empty. The main room is a mess. Clothes are scattered everywhere, old newspapers lie open across the floor, and old cups of coffee with crinkly oily surfaces sit on the ash-covered table. A long black whip curls through the rubbish, its leash like a rat's tail. I feel uneasy, as if I'm trespassing. I try to fill up the gap, her absence, with TV. The only programme on is for insomniacs: a droning Open University Physics programme. I turn on the radio, twiddle the fifties Bakelite knobs and crackle through a few stations.

Because I don't know what I want to listen to, I can't decide where to stop, so I turn it off and I'm in silence once again.

I don't do trial runs. When I finally get up and go, I go. I like to think I don't look back but it's not strictly true. I hoist myself up off the floor on to the sofa. My legs ache. My back aches. My head hurts and thuds like a hole in a gum when a tooth has been pulled out. My body feels swollen. I feel as if I've been in a car crash – every limb and bone aches.

I think of John. I think of what I've left behind. I see him waking up, face grey with stubble, finding me gone. My eyes fill with tears. I quickly pick up the paper and try to distract myself, reading the first column my eyes settle on. Instead I see John shouting out for me, getting out of bed, then blundering round the house, stumbling into furniture. 'Rue?' he'll shout. '*Rue?*' He knocks over a chair, bruises his shin. '*Rue, where are you?*' I feel guilt, then sadness, then more guilt; the emotions seem to be punching me in the stomach. I remember my mother's recipe for survival: 'Don't brood. Don't look back.' She had lived by that maxim; I don't know if I can.

A little while later when I'm in the bathroom, I catch sight of myself in the mirror. I lean on the basin and stare deep into my own eyes. This time I cry fully; great waves of sadness come and come and come and come. I take a shower and I am still crying. The tears work according to the dynamics of osmosis. The shower's droplets wring more and more of them out. I hear a clank in the lock. Anita walks into the front room and then, seeing the light is on, straight on into the bathroom.

'So you came,' she says.

I step out of the shower, wrap a stolen hotel towel round me and nod.

She puts one arm round my shoulder and then the other, and then she hugs.

'You OK?'

'No,' I reply, and out comes the truth, or my version of it – muddled, sobbing and frightened.

Infuriatingly since I'm so tired, sleep doesn't come easily. I'm trapped in a half-way state: neither asleep or awake, ticking over, processing everything that has happened like a whirring computer. 'Please God,' I go, bargaining with Him. 'Please God May Sleep Come. Please. God. Please. Please Please Please.'

When I was first working, Nina – Nina Joss Stick, we used to call her, hippie Nina – taught me a chant to sing as I fell off to sleep. 'I levitate above the bed and the world seems very small.' She used to murmur it to herself whilst her clients were pounding away on top of her.

She had some other good sayings too. 'I'm a mattress actress' was one of them. Whoever coined that phrase was a bright spark, because that's what it's all about: acting, faking. Every job starts off as an act, something detached, not quite a part of the real world.

I wrap my arms around myself and finally fall into a deep sleep. The last thing I remember is that a part of me rises above the bed and hovers over myself, like a guardian angel.

Our house. The one I've just left.

Once upon a time it was a dream house. It has a swimming pool and around the outside of the pool there are arches, and hanging from four of these arches are white muslin curtains that ripple like waves. We had a hammock in one of the arches. All around the pool there is soft green grass. And there is a long drive leading up to the front door. And I had a red MG and John had the Daimler. The flash Harry had it shipped over from Europe. And we had everything. We had everything that anyone could ever want. Sometimes I was so happy that I thought I might burst.

I dream I'm going back there. I dream I take a taxi. The cab stops at the security gates, glides up the smooth driveway, which is lined with flame trees and purple rhododendron bushes, and arrives at the white house, which transforms, at this stage of the dream, into a giant iced wedding cake.

In the morning the answering machine wakes me. When the first

7

beep goes I wait for a disembodied voice to speak out over the room's silence but no voice comes. The machine clunks and clicks and whoever it was hangs up without leaving a message.

'Does he know where you are?' Anita asks.

I shake my head. He would guess where I was but he doesn't have her number. Throughout all these years I have never mixed their company. I feared his jealousy and I feared her disdain. Anita gives men a hard time. None are ever good enough. None are ever smart enough. All are motivated solely by their dicks. Of course, she won't admit that she is as female as her enemies are male. She is the flip side of the same coin – motivated by her cunt.

'You can stay as long as you like,' she says, pouring thick treacly espresso into two chipped, filched espresso cups. 'You know that, heh?'

I remember Valentine's Day, two or three years ago. Anita and I had arranged to meet up with Julian. The streets were full of little girls holding lurid pink helium balloons shaped like hearts, the shops were full of tacky cards and Julian had succeeded in dragging us both off to the art gallery for the afternoon. It was a location that he called 'a true place for romance'.

Anita was bored from the start. She moaned about how much she wanted to sit down, about how wandering around slowly made her legs ache, about how much she wanted chocolate or coffee or both or anything.

There was one painting, full of blues of the sea and greens of the rain forest, which I still remember. Just looking at the picture made me feel alive. The past month had been bad, full of arguments with John, tough jobs at work and rip-offs. 'One day I'll fly away,' I had said dreamily, staring at the painting, and laying myself wide open for Anita's cynicism, which came as soon as I had shut my mouth. 'Oh, we all will, doll,' she had gone. 'Won't we all!' She tried to pull me down just when I was about to fly.

'What's that?' Julian had asked.

'She says she'll fly away,' Anita retorted sarkily. 'Doesn't it

8

make you sick, her virtue? Her dreams . . . don't they make you sick too?'

She pinched me on the arm as if to suggest that she didn't really mean what she was saying and that she was joking.

Julian had stuck up for me. He had poked her in the ribs and had camply flirted, telling her that she was an old wizened witch, a dried-up piece of fruit. She laughed. One of her good points is that she can take a joke at herself. Julian always smoothed out the creases. God bless him.

I remember how it had been when she had first come over. I'd known her for years. I'll go into our English past later, but for the last twelve years I had been here, on the sagging bum of the world, and she had been back home. Although she had written countless letters to say that she was on her way, I hadn't believed her. Being here, you come to expect people when they actually materialize and I hadn't honestly thought that she would.

One day there had been a call from the airport. There was no message or warning to say she was on her way, just a call from a pay box, a pause and an English accent asking directions. I had the house to myself at the time. John was in Melbourne. The new restaurant had just opened and he was tied up – giving interviews about nouvelle cuisine and white octagonal plates decorated with asparagus fern. He was becoming an, albeit minor, media celebrity, with his photo in all the glossies.

She wasn't as I had remembered her – which was full of life and always, always, full of energy. When she first arrived she had been surly, quiet and acidic. Three or four days later she had warmed up. After a week of coffees and late breakfasts spent poring over the employment section of the *Herald*, she said she needed to work.

She hadn't gone out in the evenings. She had been there when I had picked up the phone. She had heard me take down room numbers and addresses and she had watched me get dressed up and leave the house. Although she was one of my oldest friends, I hadn't dared spell out the truth. I was hoping that she would figure it out slowly, of her own accord. One morning she had clambered off the breakfast-bar stool and had said, with no fore-warning or warm-up, 'Give me the guy's number.'

'Who?' I'd gone, checking that I was reading her right.

'The guy you work for.'

'You sure?'

'Yeah,' she went. Then she said, much more softly, 'It's OK. I've thought about it.'

I pointed to the pinboard above her head. Barry's number was up there, on a card which promised 'Discreet Elite service. Service with class.' It was pinned up beside other service cards such as pool maintenance and plumbing.

She made an appointment to go and see him that night. Then she put down the handset and began to tap-dance over the tiled floor so that she sounded like a cash register.

Soon I joined in, and the two of us were clanking and clicking until we finally fell over, rolling about laughing.

A bit later she went quiet again and came up with, 'I can't.'

I wasn't going to say, 'You can', but I asked, 'Do you want to?'

And she had said, 'Yes. Yes, I do.'

We left it at that. We didn't talk about motives until months later.

Julian, the last summer that he was around, had been living in London. He was working a bit over there – not much, just the odd evening to pay for a flight over to Paris, a weekend here and a weekend there. They had met up and had spent quite a bit of time together; they had even gone to Venice for a mid-week trip. Through his company, she must have seen how he operated. She must have seen what the game required.

She knew the first rule intuitively: that it would only work for her if she went into it objectively, making a conscious decision to do it on her own terms. For a year she had kept to that rule. She was calling the shots. When the drugs had come along, and had taken centre-stage, things had changed.

I watched her come alive those early weeks. She soon had

10

enough money to find a place of her own – a shabby, ramshackle flat in a block in the Cross. She painted it all mauve – or, rather, various shades of lilac with a fuchsia-pink sofa. It was an eyesore choice, but that's Anita.

We used to open the balcony windows, push her heavy oak table to the side of the room, put on some loud African music and dance and sing.

We would dance for an hour or so, without stopping. We would just move and sway and move and sway and move and sway.

It was easy then. Life seemed effortless, like lying in the cool shade of a fig tree or under the spreading boughs of an avocado tree. I would say like lying in the sun, only these are the nineties and when I think sun I think slip-slop-slap and corny government health warnings, and when I think sun I think cancer. When I think sex I sometimes think the same. I try not to, but in the back of my mind the link is always there, the age-old link between sex and death.

I come back to Julian and the others and that chrome-railed balcony in the hospice where, at the end, we sipped peppermint tea and he sat shivering although it was a hot Sydney summer. The view we looked out on to was where it had happened in the beginning – the wall in Darlinghurst, lined with white-jeaned rent boys and humming with hovering flash cars.

2

Anita has a client due to arrive at three, so I go out at two to make way for him. Before I leave, I call the agency and tell them that I won't be working tonight or this afternoon. I don't tell Barry the reason, which is that I can't stand the thought of any dick's dick inside me today and that just today I don't want to be invaded, but I give him some excuse about bleeding. Barry pauses. I panic: I might have used that excuse too many times before. Baz is a kink; he probably keeps a diary with every woman's cycle marked out inside it. Next he will accuse me of being a biological freak or a liar.

He doesn't. He just says, 'Getting unreliable, Ruby . . . You know what happens to girls like you . . .'

'Oh, I'll probably turn into a frog or a pumpkin or a piece of old cheese,' I reply. I think the cheese bit is good, but he misses his cue for repartee and there is a lengthy silence.

Barry isn't on my wavelength; he isn't on any wavelength at all. He plods along on surfaces. He is a ground man. Sometimes I think he might even be a termite – a small, ugly, colourless woodlouse.

'Hello?' I go, checking to see if he is still there.

Although he won't knee-cap me if I don't do the job, he is a headfucker and I have to work hard not to be sucked in. He chunders out a familiar spiel: this is the last job I'll be offered this week, business is slack and, lastly, I'm no spring chicken and I should be lucky that anyone still wants me. I am thirty-three.

I hold the phone out to the wall until his stupid burble stops. I won't begin to play his game. Then I address him with a fiercer determination than ever before – a crystalline precision.

'I'll call you when I'm ready to work.'

I stress the 'I'. To some this might be a small point but for me it's a large one. I am trying to use more of these small, egocentric touches. I hang up before I get time to hear his reply.

At two I go out, buy a *Herald* and take it to an empty, nearby café. I take the best seat there is, beside the french windows, half outside on the pavement. I order a café latte from a waitress whose apron ties dig into her waist like elastic round a soft cushion. I unfold the paper and scan the accommodation columns. My red felt-tip pen hovers, ready to pounce on a possibility. Nowhere sounds possible.

The next port of call is an estate agent. A chap called Guy drives me round to view a few flats in Rushcutters Bay. We go up lifts and into empty apartments where the air smells stagnant and where the surfaces are clean yet dusty. We go down lifts and out on to grey, flat car-parks. 'No,' I say. Guy seems surprised. The flat I've just turned down has a sixteenth-floor harbour view and is going for a dime. I didn't like the carpet. It was gold and red and swirling, and the block had seemed too quiet, full of retired folk. The whole place was too twilight and not enough midday.

Finally I escape Guy by promising to rifle through the wedge of details he has given me. I'm bushwhacked, tired to the bones. I walk down to the small patch of grass at the end of Victoria Street and sit on the green. From here I can see the docks. A ship is in from Russia, another from Argentina and a navy ship from the US. Trolleys come and go, cranes move slowly up and down against the blue sky and a couple of marines walk along the Dockside to check in at one end of a makeshift Wimpy office and to check out the other side. I lie back and fall asleep. I dream of toy town, of magic roundabouts and toy shops, of dolls'-houses and Matchbox cars, of dolls that cry and dolls that talk. When I wake up it's six thirty and dusk is falling, and I discover that I'm an adult. I am flesh, bones, 70 per cent water and, despite all odds, I have everything intact.

When I reach Anita's flat, the front door is unusually open and the radio is on in the background, playing some tacky un-cred music that she wouldn't normally bother with. She isn't in the living room and the dungeon door is closed. Four hours have gone by since her client must have arrived and at maximum one since he must have left. I stand at the door and cock an ear. I can hear nothing. I shout out her name. No one replies. Usually, even if she was in the middle of a session, she would shout out a 'Yes'. I'm puzzled but I leave it, go through to the kitchen and make some tea. Then I shout again. Still no answer comes. I think long and hard and finally decide to go in.

She is sprawled out on the floor, half under the bed, surrounded by the remnants of a session: black and pink dildos, bum plugs, purple latex Japanese vibrators, electric toothbrushes, nylon and string ropes, chains, whips, leashes, wigs and six-inch spikes. At first I suppose that she hasn't bothered to lift herself up on to the bed and that she is simply half asleep, half-awake – collapsed in a heap exactly where the session ended. When she doesn't react to my presence, I say her name. She doesn't reply; I panic.

Her thin body is limp like a rag doll. I shake it. There's no elasticity in it. She moans.

'O Christ Christ Jesus Christ, Christ Jesus God God Please Please Help' I think as I rush to the phone and dial emergency.

We are half a mile away, no more, from a hospital. The ambulance arrives within minutes. Her tiny, frail body is wrapped up inside a scarlet blanket, bundled inside the screaming car and whisked away. They also take the syringe that they find stuffed into the soft flesh of a grapefruit which has rolled down under the bed and has thick, grey, blobs of dust stuck to it.

I follow by foot and stay at the hospital until it is absolutely clear that she'll pull through. She will pull through; she always does. There have been near scrapes before and each time she springs back up again, defiant, like a weed in a garden sprayed with weedkiller. I chain-drink tea in the waiting room. Finally a friendly nurse (all teeth, smiles and Greek-widow, thick black tights) bustles out. 'You can go now,' she says. 'She's fine.'

Right now I feel I don't have the reserves to deal with this.

What pools of strength that I possess, I need for me. Yet I feel selfish, as if I should be at her bedside, if not tonight, then at least first thing tomorrow morning. I should be issuing advice, counselling, making good, smoothing.

Instead, when I do get to see her, I give her a hard time. I don't intend to do this; it's what comes out. 'You're still doing this shit?' I say.

It is three days later and she is sitting propped up in a hospital bed, looking sparkily healthy, getting the nurses to do this and that, bring this food here, take away that food there, turn on the TV to that station. 'Sometimes,' she answers.

She does it when she needs to blank out. She needs to blank out in order to work. We end up arguing. From my side, I can't bear to see her do this to herself.

'Fuck, Ruby . . . all you can do is play school ma'am with me. I'm in hospital. I had an accident and this is the shit I get. Fuck off. Fuck right off.'

'OK, OK, OK,' I go, stepping backwards, taking my leave, feeling I have gone too far.

'Hey,' she says, when I have reached the door. 'Sorry. I'm sorry.'

On about the third day of looking, by this time without Guy, I find a house. It's in Glebe, a suburb that is a long way away from where the white house was. I prefer it here. The area isn't so suburban and anaesthetized. The house is an end of row. It has a tin roof, a peppercorn tree in the garden and a quiet suburban back lane that runs the length of the terrace. In comparison to the white house, this one is a shoebox – two up, two down.

I love the back lane. I love the feel of the hot sun as it belts down and bounces off the cracked dry ground. I love the sounds; how right in the heart of the city I can hear cicadas. I love the silence too; the heat muffles the noise of traffic. It soaks it up like bread and gravy.

When I'm not bustling about – off up to the hospital to see Anita, off to Glebe to put down deposits, off swimming obsessive lengths in the pool – I think about John. Sometimes it can feel as if I have just severed off my arm.

'Get out of my head, John,' I whisper under my breath one afternoon. I'm on a bus, going down Macquarie Street, past the hospital. It begins to rain and the rain falls so hard that the bus is forced to pull over and halt until the worst of the torrent is over and the driver can see out of the front window once more. John has reappeared in my memory, in soft and soapy focus. He is cooking me chicken soup when I was ill. He is phoning in twice a day from Melbourne to see if I am worse or better. He is simply smiling. He is happy.

I try desperately to make him 100 per cent monster. I try to focus on the way he'd disappear for two nights, then show up and we'd fuck and fuck and fuck and I would open up like a sea anemone. Once he had possessed me, he'd be off, disappear again – into the great unknown.

I keep thinking back to the start. I felt taken care of. I think of his cock. I think of how well he used it and how ignition like that happens rarely, once in a lifetime. I spin myself a sob story. Love won't happen again. I had my chance and I messed it up.

Once she is home Anita convinces me that it was an accident, the result of an encounter with a particularly testing client, and that she has a lust for life which can't be quelled and that, therefore, it is perfectly all right for me to move out as soon as possible.

What makes me believe her hymn to life is that she paints the living-room walls bright red. She explains that this is all part of the plan to re-energize herself and that for a fortnight the only food she will eat will also be red. She whacks down a crumpled envelope on the table in front of me upon which is scrawled every type of red food that she can think up: red kidney beans, strawberries, tomatoes, red peppers, plums, beetroot, raspberry yoghurt, cherry pie. She shows me the list absolutely seriously and absolutely enthusiastically.

Despite her crankiness I am relieved, because I deduce that if she had been intent on leaving she would have chosen brown, and it's true, she does seem to be full of life. She doesn't strike me as being someone opting out, about to fade away like the voices from a radio whose plug has just been pulled out from the mains.

17

3

I lived in a shabby little flat in south London whose back garden overlooked the railway line. The windows shook and quivered all night long and the grass in the scrubby little garden was always grey, shrouded with concrete dust. I hated it there. I hated what went on inside the house; the noise of shouts from the flat above, the radio from the room above, the arguments. I hated what went on outside too. There was nowhere pleasant to play, nothing was clean and even the trees were dirty and grew polythene-bag leaves.

We met in an accident. It wasn't exactly a motorway pile-up, replete with sirens and ambulances; it was a child's accident and it involved speed and someone being run over. I had been given a new bicycle, a navy-blue Raleigh sit up and beg, a gift from Geoff, and I was swirling down the pavement on it, looping round the cracks between the paving stones, when she darted out of her driveway, straight into my path. I skidded, braked, and knocked her down. *'Fuck you!'* she bellowed. This was suburbia in the sixties. Divorce was a dirty word; Sunday school was not. A few grey, grimy lace curtains began to twitch.

Anita's Mum, Deirdre, a big burly Liverpudlian lady, rushed out of the house to see what was going on. By that time I was up and away, unlatching our green wooden gate.

The next afternoon there had been a timid knock at the door. I was reading, tucked away in a corner of my bedroom, squashed between the bed and a wall. No one else was at home. I immediately thought that it might be Geoff's brother, Alan, come to deliver the weekly groceries. Instead it was Anita, standing meekly in the doorway and fiddling nervously with gold cross

18

which hung around her neck. 'I'm sorry,' she said, offering a posy of summer flowers whose stems were bound in creased silver foil, the way that gypsies bind heather.

'I shouldn't have said those words. God will punish me. Or He would have done if I hadn't said my Hail Marys. Do you want to come to the park? I'm a Catholic.'

She rounded up her sentence by blowing a large pink bubble. It burst and it smelt of fruit.

I needed friends. Because I was never allowed to reciprocate invitations and ask people back to the house, I didn't have many. I liked the idea of having a friend who was also a neighbour, although, as she stood in the worn-away dent of the doorstep, I was scared of her. She wasn't normal.

'OK,' I finally went.

Her eyes were slightly askew and they were an odd colour – a shade of lilac that I've never seen on anyone else. Her hair was carrot orange; it was red for danger.

I was eleven and she must have just turned nine. That summer we went to the park every afternoon and always followed the same routine. I would scratch around for insects which I would hand to her and she would sit under the spreading boughs of an oak tree and slowly dissect what I had given her. 'Dolls are dull, don't you think?' she would say, peeling the wing from a wasp or the leg off an ant. I didn't agree but I nodded and watched the gory operation avidly. Secretly I had a store of dolls in my bedroom. 'Know what I'd like to do?' she went on. 'I'd like to steal every doll belonging to every girl in my class and build a bonfire and burn them.' This was summer 1968.

'Do you like boys?' This time we were on the top floor of a red double-decker which was chugging up Ludgate Hill to St Paul's like an old woman. We were meeting Deirdre for a day out.

'No,' I said. I didn't. They terrified me.

'I do,' she had said, licking a raspberry lolly.

'You don't like them because you think they're all like Geoff. Mum says you should run away. She says it's not right.'

'What's not right?'

19

'The way he . . . you know.'

She blushed and wouldn't go on.

I didn't help her out. I was under oath and Geoff was a big man. I had seen his anger taken out on my mother and I was prepared to keep any amount of silence to prevent that from happening to me.

I left Wandsworth as soon as I could. I just packed my bags and went, the first of a series of barely explained exits. I spent a year going from one lover to the next – getting through men like cigarettes, or fixes, until I met Ray. Throughout those years I was pulling pints, living in squats, signing on, waitressing, stripping, I kept in touch with Anita, who, by now, had become the only family I had.

I left in the late seventies. The sixties were long gone and no spirit had moved fully into their place. London was meandering, drifting like a chiffon scarf. I left for good. I wanted heat. Above all, I wanted to be as far away as possible.

I don't want to go into the ins and outs of Geoff. Suffice it to say that he wore a lot of brown Courtelle. The colour brown, Thames mud brown, surrounded him. All the clothes that he wore were brown. All the gifts that he gave – mugs, gloves, socks – were brown.

He was my mother's second husband – my stepfather. They married when I was seven. He had no children of his own; I was his only one, and I was that by proxy. He sat behind a newspaper all day long and later, when we got a TV, he would sit in front of that and he would watch any junk that came on, anything. He was a *Crossroads* addict. From the day that he arrived, when I hoped I might have a dad to play with, to look up to, to admire, he was always there, static in the front room like an unwelcoming, hard-backed wooden chair.

He had an excuse for his inactivity – back problems. He couldn't work because if he over-exerted himself his spine would jam and then he would have to spend a month immobile, flat on his back on the floor like a dead man. If this happened we would have to tiptoe around him and bring him tea and cosset.

Mum saw to the bills. Mum's real name was Betty. She did an odd day here, at the corner shop, selling sherbet fountains and gobstoppers, tallying up on a clunky old pounds, shillings and pence cash register, and she did the odd day there, in a dental practice, working as a receptionist.

Those one-offs wouldn't have been enough. There was another side to her life which she hid from me as a child but which I discovered about later, years after I had left home. I am remembering her long trips into town on weekday afternoons, dolled up to the Bette Lynch nines. I am remembering the 'treats' that might follow one of those trips – a new dress, a new toy, wine for dinner. I am remembering the purr of a black taxi in the street outside as it pulled up to drop her off. Mum saw to the bills. I had precedents for my line of work: like mother, like daughter.

I want to ask her, 'Why did you marry him?' but I can't. I would be speaking into thin air, into the wind. Mum passed over fifteen years ago, a few months after I had met John. By the time anyone told me the news of her death the funeral was over and gone. I was cheated of a goodbye.

She settled with Geoff because he was always there and he wouldn't go away. He couldn't leave her; he was just glued to his chair, or later to his thin cane walking stick. Before she met him she had spent years on her own and the loneliness was beginning to overwhelm her. Geoff was the first man to come along after she had reached this low point of isolation and despair. He was the first bus to stop and she climbed on board without really thinking too much about the destination. Geoff was dependent on her in every way and I loathed him. I despised him his dependence.

Mum, about the other. How much? How often? With whom?

My real father, Jack Tanner, left when I was two. Hearsay has it that he packed his bags, walked out of the door, left no forwarding address and was never heard of again. After he went Mum burnt every picture that existed of him, tipped out all his possessions on to the street on rubbish-collection day so that dogs pissed on them, and moved house. Mum didn't mess about. We were out within a week, off into a new life, moving from Bromley to south London.

When questioned, she would say two things about Jack Tanner, and even then they revealed more about her character than they did about his. One: 'I loved him.' Two: 'I burnt for him.'

I often asked about this vacuum of a man. His lack of identity made him especially appealing and especially romantic. Soon I got wise to Mum's responses, and when I mentioned his name I would feed her the lines before she spoke them; I'd do a kind of double-act. 'I burnt for him,' I remember saying, nine years old, legs dangling off the end of the Formica kitchen peninsula, hands diving into the yellow tupperware biscuit box. I wondered what the hell it meant to 'burn' for someone; it sounded painful and something to be avoided at all costs. Somehow the thought of Mum burning for anyone didn't match up with who I saw her to be. In my eyes she was strong and almost indomitable.

I have been looking for him all my life. My search for him, between the thighs of many men, cradled in their arms, reflected in their eyes, is this story. It's an old story, old as hills and rocks and mountains, older far than trees. You don't have to be a shrink to see that it is any woman's story. But it is especially ours; it belongs especially to us working women.

His absence, this father that never was, left a well which I filled and filled indiscriminately with any liquid on offer. However much I filled it, it was never full and there was never enough.

One day, it must have been after I had met John because I remember we were in Vaucluse, in the flat overlooking the sea (you could hear it roaring from the bed, crashing on the rocks below), Anita phoned. She never bothered to work out the hour differences and she always seemed genuinely surprised to discover there was a time difference at all between southern and northern hemispheres. She seemed to believe that she was exempt from such things. I was asleep. It was four in the morning.

She had moved out of Wandsworth and she was living in a

shared house in Camden. She was dealing dope in a haphazard kind of way, and had a market stall every Sunday where she sold big vulgar glasses and bowls and ash trays – fifties glassware shaped like female genitalia.

She came straight out with the news. She never wasted time on party chat and, besides which, she was paying, feeding a telephone kiosk fifty-pence pieces.

'Mum's come over. Want to hear some good news? Geoff is dead. "D" for Dog, "E" for Egg, "A" for Ant and "D" for Dog again. God backwards. Died last week.'

For years Anita had been the only person who knew the secret. Right at the end, a fortnight of so ago, I told John, but it was only when I felt that I had nothing to lose and that there wasn't a relationship to save, and when I felt that he couldn't point a finger at me and treat me as having been part to blame. I thought it might help to explain the mess we were in. It didn't. Or, at least, not outright, but I wished that I had shared this stuff earlier, because he was soft and tender and accepting – not at all what I had expected, which was rigid and judgemental.

When I heard that Geoff had died an electric current rippled through my body. I leapt in the air and whooped for joy. Even when I didn't know where he was, I had been living with the fear that one day he might track me down and maybe even kill me for what I knew about him. I thought he might come to get me like the bogeyman. Now, at last, I felt safe. I put down the phone and fell asleep again and slept until dusk.

When I met John, at the start, I was seventeen going on almost eighteen and I had, as I now see is entirely usual, no idea of what I was going to do.

I had left Ray, my first love, earlier in the afternoon. I see him now, lying in that squalid council flat in Hackney, propped up against an ochre-yellow wall, saying, with rich West Indian inflections, 'If you only learn one thing from me, Julie, learn this.'

I listened to him intently, as I had done for the past year or so. The phone started ringing. We were in bed. He leant across my body, picked up the receiver and dropped it back into the cradle without speaking. Then he promptly took it off the hook.

'Fate's like a mistress, babe.'

I smiled. By then I had learnt that smiles usually buy time.

'And if you do this, she'll take care of you.'

'What, Ray? Tell me. Tell me.'

I had learnt to pander and to tease, to play up to the teacher role that he sometimes inadvertently adopted. He was twenty years older than I was. He had taught me and I had learnt from him.

'Court her. Pamper her like a mistress. Feed her on freedom. Then – only then – she'll take you to her soft breasts and she'll rock you like a baby. Remember that, JuJu.'

At the time I had thought he was a pompous git. He was. But somewhere in the middle of the pomp, he sometimes got things right. He was right about fate. 'Be open to come what may and ride on the tide.' Even now I believe his philosophy.

I left Ray on the understanding that I would return when I had finished whatever it was that I had to do, which, in retrospect, was simply to escape. If I had stayed there, in that flat, I would have grown old with him years before my time. I didn't say this to him. It would have seemed cruel; besides which I was only groping at the truth then. I only half saw it.

The trick is, wherever, whenever, to get on the road and to keep walking without stopping and without looking back.

It was later that same day that I met John. A car pulled up – a silvery, birch-green Jaguar XJS. Up till then my knowledge of cars had been limited to leaking tin cans which had to be kick-started on frosty winter mornings. Inside this machine, which glided and purred and waited on the pavement like a cat about to pounce, was a devilishly handsome man.

He was tall, well built, with big bones and pale-green eyes, and he must have been nearing forty. He had wavy light-brown hair and an olive-skinned, chiselled face which was bony, with no spare flesh. His handsome looks didn't quite add up. His roman nose was too big and ended in a round knob which hung over

24

his top lip, there was a gap between his two front teeth, and when he was tired his eyes seemed to be off-centre and they almost, but not quite, looked in different directions. Right from the moment I saw him I sensed tangibly (my body tingled) his magnetism. There was something about him that was irresistible, and what it was was a confidence rather than an arrogance, and a suggestion in the way he walked, confidently and calmly, that he had been everywhere his desire or imagination had led him and that he wouldn't deny any experience. He was a six-foot-tall magnet and I was a dancing iron filing.

He was still working for his father, Pa Goldman, in the delicatessen business, where he sold gravalax, smoked salmon, herrings and kosher meatballs. He was living in St John's Wood, in a flat painted dark green, the colour of German pine forests, and he was driving past the Regent on his way home from work. It was a Friday evening. I was sitting opposite the hotel's entrance, perched on the top of a bashed-up old leather suitcase.

The traffic was thick, bumper to boot, and the exhaust fumes had created a knee-deep layer of fog which hovered over the road like a thirteen-tog duvet. It was twilight – too early for every car to have its headlights on. I stuck my thumb out. I was feeling cheeky, I just flung it out in the middle of the road, never really thinking anything would come of it, not here in stuffy, central London any rate. He wound down the window and beckoned me to come over.

I got up and walked nonchalantly over to the car. I leant my elbows against the clunky door and stuck my arse up in the air.

'Where do you want to go?' he asked.

'Anywhere. You say.'

'Get in.'

I did.

We drove down to Oxfordshire and ended up going beyond the city with its dreaming spires which pierced the sky like silver knitting needles until we reached the Cotswolds.

On the journey down, we didn't talk. I sank back into the leather seat and inhaled the smells of leather and mahogany

25

polish. I became acutely aware of the car's movements, of its gaining and losing speed, of the curves and inclines in the road. I wallowed in sensation. I remember shutting my eyes so that I could pretend that I was asleep when really I was wide awake all the time.

We finally arrived in a dinky little town where John knew of a hotel. The hotel was calculatedly English, twee enough to pull in the American tourists, of whom there were many, and comfortable enough to keep them there. It took us a whole week to have sex. The fact that it took so long seemed to reinforce my sense of destiny about the affair. I wanted to believe that this was meant to be. I wanted to believe that this had been written in the stars. I wanted to believe that we were special. I wanted to believe that the gods were on our side.

Over dinner the first night he asked my name. At that stage we still hadn't exchanged details. 'Julie,' I replied. He winced – pulling his mouth down at either side of his face into a 180-degree straight line. 'Change it,' he said. 'Change it and stay.'

Along with fate, or the belief that this was meant to happen, I wanted to believe something else: I wanted to believe in the strength and power of others. I fell for his air of authority. I blew up what little strength there was in his character to grandiose proportions. I did well: I managed to pull wool over my own eyes. That initial fortnight was all about falling in love with an illusion, with a person who I willed to be there but who wasn't, a person who was in fact thin, like smoke or a ghost.

From the start I had seen Ray clearly – so clearly that I couldn't add a fantasy to what was. The contrast of where I had come from – the dingy flat in Hackney – to where I was now was huge. By the time we drove back into London and slid over the Westway late one night, as if the road were a silk ribbon rippling beneath us, I was completely in love with John. The whole experience – meeting him the way I did, the hotel, the luxury – was enormous enough, and novel enough, for me to tumble for him 100 per cent. I had swallowed a hook and I spent the next fifteen years attached to a line. Every time I tried to swim free, I would rip the soft flesh in the back of my throat so that the pain of leaving kept me there.

I often think that all relationships are like blocks of ice held in the palm of a hand. The hotter the hand the faster they melt. Or take it further: imagine a slab of ice like a chunk of crystal on a black tarmacked road. Imagine a blazing petrol can, flames licking the blue sky, right next to it. We were both those things, both the fire and the ice.

4

Being around Anita when she started working took me back to when I was doing the same. It was in London, three months after I had met John, and we were living in St John's Wood.

The fact was that I had to make a living. The fact was that I always rise to a challenge. The fact was that I wanted whole fat, bagel-ridden days, when I could be a lazy doll and loll around doing nothing in particular. The fact was that it suited John to have me hook. In a weird way, working made me depend on him. I needed his support. I needed him to say that it was OK and that I would be all right. At the start he was good at giving reassurance. He wanted to give it. He needed that dependence and our needs, to give and to receive, created a perfect circle.

A friend of John's, Jenny, was hooking, and I met her, talked to her and it didn't seem such a bad deal. The money was good, the hours short, and once you'd mastered how to whore, well, the world was your oyster. I talked about it over and over to John. He didn't have any serious objections. Needs apart, maybe it was even fulfilling one of his fantasies, though if that was the case, he was never honest about it. Finally I called the number Jenny had given me and the same evening, dressed in my best clothes and underwear, I took a cab to the apartment block where the agency was based.

If I was going to do it, I would lose my London accent and do it from the top. VIP had a smart address in Knightsbridge. The apartment was a penthouse suite and it overlooked the park. A woman named Sarah opened the door. She was a sultry, olive-skinned woman in her early thirties: dark-haired, lush-looking, immaculately turned out in muted Italian linens and French silks.

She was holding a tiny baby who lay on her lap all the way through the interview. Sarah wasn't what I imagined anyone working in the sex industry to look like. I had imagined someone tawdry and overstated. She seemed refined – a smooth-edged seductress.

She led me into a small, plushly decorated office. She sat down behind a large, mock-antique desk and motioned that I relax into the black leather sofa opposite, from where I had a view of the wintry park. Occasionally the phone would go and she would answer it, rattle through girls' statistics and make bookings. She told me that she had worked herself, though not any longer; 'It's not right with the baby.'

After we had been through all the details – how much, what was expected of me, what type of underwear I'd need – she led me through to meet the boss, Mike.

He was sitting in what was obviously his living room. He had the TV on, with the volume turned down, and he was watching racing results. The room was as expensively decorated as Sarah's office had been, with huge leather sofas, exotic Deco lamps (naked ladies twisted around tree trunks) and Chinese vases. Put together, the design details gave the place a feeling of opulence. On the wall, over the fireplace, was a painting of racehorses galloping to the finish of the race. Mike was reclining, a large Scotch beside him.

I never liked Mike. Life had dealt him a rotten hand and it was the same hand that he tried to deal out to everyone else. He was bitter and angry. He was in his fifties: a small man, slightly built, with a paunch and a gold chain and St Christopher round his neck. Like Geoff, Mike always dressed in shades of brown and his clothes always needed a good press. Everything he wore had creases in it: a creased tan-coloured shirt, creased tan trousers.

Sarah muttered an introduction and then scurried out of the room. Mike stayed seated, slowly eyeing me up. Then he stood up and walked over to me so that his face was about five inches away from mine.

'Bowels regular?'

I nodded.

'You're all bound up. Drink garlic water.'

He pinched my cheeks.

'Where are the cheekbones?'

I was standing with my back to the wall and he moved closer so that his body was pressing into mine. I felt challenged, semi-invaded.

'You know how to excite a man?'

'I think so.'

'Not good enough, "think".'

I snapped back at him this time. I couldn't stand there and take it, an empty jug, any more.

'Of course I fucking know.'

He backed off, momentarily silenced.

'That's no way to get a job, lady. Not with that kind of attitude. I'm doing you a favour – remember?'

Then he put his hands on my breasts and squeezed them very hard, so roughly that it hurt.

'Where are they?'

I didn't answer. I wasn't going to get them out and flash them on like car headlights. Jenny had warned me of the power game that he would try to play. Once a woman is hired (and they usually are), a pimp running an agency doesn't have any real power over a hooker. He is outside of the action, a go-between. Pimps know this and they hate it. This impotence, I figured, was the reason for his attempt to dominate now.

'Look at you. You could be stunning. What's happened? Want to be a lazy whore like all the others? . . . You could use this to set yourself up – earn twenty grand in six months. Use it. Hear me. Use it. Look at you. You're a mess. Cheap clothes. No money. Fake pearls. What a fucking waste. What a waste.'

'You going to hire me or not?'

He eyed me up again and nodded slowly, toying with an imaginary goatee on the end of his chin.

'I'll hire you, and the next time we meet I'll be sober and we'll have a glass of white wine and I won't mention any of this.'

30

He laughed and assumed a mock Brideshead accent. 'Of course, I can be quite a gentleman.'

'Is that it?' I asked.

He didn't answer but moved towards me, grabbed my face and tried to push his tongue between my closed lips.

'Want a job now?' he grunted.

Jenny had warned me of how he liked to test out his workers. Frequently he would phone women up in the middle of the night and ask them to go over. Once he had sent a limo to collect Jenny and to take her to a supposedly regular job. When she arrived at the booking, way out of town, she had been expecting to meet a Mr X. Instead it was Mike who had swung open the door, grinning slyly. There had been no Mr X involved at all. Jenny had been trapped.

'Bet your boyfriend doesn't tell you any of that stuff about yourself, does he? Nah. Coz you know why? . . . It's the truth. He wouldn't dare.'

I let myself out. I went home. I showered.

The next day I called up Sarah. The next night I was working.

The ones who run the show and pick up percentages are all shits. They know they're shits and they try to avoid what they know about themselves by convincing us that we can't live without them. If you let one of them get inside your head he'll mash it up like potato.

5

Of course I want to give it up, that goes for granted. But until it feels right to move on, until I know where I'm heading, I'll stay raking in the cash like dead leaves in an autumn park, and try to keep myself to myself and not to give too much away. This keeping myself to myself, a kind of psychic celibacy, that's what's hard. I give give give. Then I resent resent resent.

The first night I go back to work, I do two jobs. Both are with fat, balding regulars who have been waiting for me to come back on call. It's good to see the first one. He is easy – all I have to do is pump up and down and watch TV. The other, from Taiwan, is hard work. 'Do this. Do that. Not that – this! . . . More! . . . Turn over!' Nothing is the way he wants it and I come away drained.

The following night I do a job which starts out easy but which turns on me gradually like a pint of slowly souring milk.

He is a managing director of a pharmaceuticals firm in Switzerland and he is in Sydney for a conference. Like most of them he says he never has sex with his wife. He's civil, clean and regular, like a white bap with a regular, no frills, burger.

After we have done it – nothing fancy, straight up, straight down – he begins to cry. He rolls over on his side and tries to hide his distress but he doesn't manage it. Everything spills out, like double cream splurging out of a carton over a carpet: his life history, his marriage (held together for the children's sake), his moral qualms about holding the position he does. Recently his dog was kidnapped. When he refused to pay the ransom money, the dog was delivered dead on his doorstep. Now he is racked with guilt at his heartlessness. Listening to him, I assume a different role: therapist-cum-mother.

I hold him in my arms and rock him as if he is a child. Then I run a bubble bath and scrub his back, and after two hours are up I tuck him up and kiss him on his cheek goodbye.

Standing in the hotel portico, watching the porter flash the CAB NEEDED sign out on the street, I'm angry at myself that after fifteen years I am still unable to switch off like, I imagine, other women can. Although I can't remember the Swiss man's name, his story is inside me and its telling was part of a one-sided transaction – one in which my personality was constantly hidden, one in which I was constantly absent.

Back in my flat, I switch on the radio and tune in. Anita's voice drifts out over the warm city. It moves gently, like algae wafting in the water of a rockpool, or long hair in a bath. She has a voice to get hooked to – low-toned, soothing and clammy.

'Honey. Honey. Honey,' she says.

It is way after midnight. She must be alone in the studio. She prefers to work in the dark; there will be no overhead lights on. I see the glow of a cigarette's end – warm, warm red, like the glow of bonfire embers and I see the green streaks of the sound-machine monitor trickle up and down with the crescendos of her voice. There are some lads about somewhere, technicians in the studio above, but she can't see them. She is in the dark womb of her studio. 'Honey. Honey. Honey,' she says.

A woman calls in, names herself Dot and starts to cry. Her husband has gone off with some other woman, a mistress of ten years' standing, a woman he has even had a kid with. He has kept the mistress and the child a secret from his wife all along. Suddenly the bubble has burst and the wife has phoned up tonight. It's two thirty, towards the end of the shift. The woman begins to talk about suicide. Anita hates ending on a bad note; she closes down and keeps the woman on the line. She probably even swaps home numbers in case the woman feels sore later on in the night. Anita is soft like that – an easy touch if you know where to touch which corner of the heart, not the whole heart, but an angle of it; she's soft flesh with a hard shell.

The show closes and a jazz programme begins. I'm still buzzing

– part anger, part caffeine, part general unease – and the slow, wandering horn music aggravates my tetchiness rather than calms it. I switch off the radio, take a shower and try to wash the mood and client away.

When I first started working I spent whole half-days in the bath, with the door locked behind me so that John wouldn't march in. Anywhere and everywhere he would march in unannounced. His step was proprietorial. He believed he owned everything around him. He believed with authority. He always had this authority.

After ten minutes the water runs cold, so I get out. It's now four in the morning and dawn is breaking. At first the odd bird is singing and within five to ten minutes all the birds in the trees have joined in and are squawking at top volume. I toss and turn for an hour or so. I can't sleep. I feel as if I just can't be alone. I phone up Anita. 'Come on over . . .' she goes, 'Can't sleep either.'

Sometimes after a particularly isolating job, one in which I felt dead inside, I couldn't go home and share a bed with John. I didn't want to take what I had just been through and put any of it on to him. He was someone and somewhere apart and I wanted him to stay that way – separate and untainted.

There is a saying amongst us workers – 'We carry a community in our hearts.' We are family.

When I first started working there was Nina. She knew about the perspective that a hooker acquires which separates and isolates her. It was a perspective that I couldn't discuss with John, not only because he wouldn't understand, but also because, as time went on, there were traces of jealousy when I mentioned work and it was far easier to keep what happened on a job to myself, to zip up my lips, rather than to suffer the sulks and the moods. Gradually my silences spread into other areas of my life too. I didn't tell him about the man who, only a month ago, had pulled a knife, fucked me, and left me in a motel 30 kilometres outside Sydney, without paying and without the fare home. The public wouldn't understand how a hooker can get raped on a job and nor would John.

Nina had been through what I was stepping into. She knew that the more jobs a hooker does, the more she begins to understand that nothing really matters and that everything comes round again, in a circle.

We used to go up to the office every Thursday to sort out business details with Mike – to collect any money owed us from credit-card transactions and to pay him back the third we owed him from cash jobs. Unless I had done a ménage or something special, like a meal out with a bunch of clients, it was the only time that I got to meet the other girls. One afternoon, sitting on the leather sofa in a queue with three other girls in front of me, I met Nina. She was haggling over twenty quid with Mike, who sat with what must have been three grand in cash stacked in front of him. Finally, after a quarter of an hour's haggling, he gave it to her. We left at the same time, took the lift down to the ground floor, went to Harrods' food hall, bought a picnic and went to the park for the afternoon. We soon made it a habit after Thursday pay days to meet up.

Nina was twenty-seven and had been working on and off for three years. In the off-years she had travelled – to India, South America, and more glamorously to Paris and Rome. She spoke with a middle-class accent, had been to university and said she wanted one thing out of life – to have as big an adventure as possible, and to be paid for it.

Those first months when I needed all the tips I could get, her moral support was a huge bonus. Some nights we would meet up after work and would go out together. Some nights we would meet up in the swimming pools of the big hotels where we had been working and we would pretend that we were guests.

After a year she went to work in New York.

We kept in touch. Things were going well for her. She had an apartment on West 78th Street and she was attending a school of journalism. She met a man through work, a banker, who she was living with and she said she felt happier than ever before.

35

A couple of months after that letter I received another one, this one signed Jacob King. Nina had been killed on a job. The letter didn't go into details but there was a phone number which I called. I spoke to Jacob direct.

It had been a routine job at the Hilton. The guy had been shooting coke into his arm and his gear was out when there had been a knock at the door. The guy hadn't worried; he had thought it was a friend staying in the next-door room, come to ask Nina to do a second job after she was finished with this one. Instead it was the drug squad and Nina's client was a key cocaine dealer. Buzzing and whirring after the injection, he had panicked, grabbed a gun from the bedside table drawer and had shot. He had missed the cop but the bullet had ricocheted hitting Nina in the chest. That had been on Friday night. She died on the Sunday morning.

'So,' Jacob had said in an East Coast drawl (a classy drawl, definitely Harvard), 'you girls can never be too careful. Got the message? Quit!'

For a fortnight after that I did quit. I wanted to think about her and I wanted to reassess. I felt pretty numbed as much by her early death as by its cause. I had always known of the dangers but survival instinct meant that I hadn't let them in; I hadn't dwelt on them. I had believed that trouble came to the bubbleheads, the girls who went to a job and bled it, in terms of drugs and alcohol, for all it was worth. Accidents came to those whose sixth sense was temporarily on hold. They couldn't sniff a rat; they couldn't run as soon as their noses started to twitch.

Nina's dream showed that it could happen to anyone. She was a smart and sober worker. She was the one who taught me to stand near the door until I got an overview of the punter. She was the one who taught me to ask for unusual ID such as membership cards from libraries, or gyms, rather than easily fudged credit cards. Her death showed me, for the first time, that I was playing with fire. The fact that I went back to work after only a fortnight, willingly chose to return, showed me that I couldn't relinquish playing with fire and that, in some way, I was as hooked to the job as, by this stage, I was hooked to John.

'I'm glad you came over,' Anita says, as we collapse back into the springless old sofa and she switches off the video – a teach-yourself Italian programme which she is trying to learn as and when she remembers to. Outside it is a sunny six a.m. Round the corner, down on William Street, the dawn trucks rumble and shudder past on their way out of Sydney. The walls of the flat vibrate.

'I could really do with some ordinary human contact,' Anita says. 'Do you ever get that? Just ordinary life? Mugs of tea, soap operas?'

Often I dream of a house in suburbia. I yearn for a sprinkler on the lawn, 2.5 kids, a dust-free kitchen and a faithful husband with a modest income. It's an absurd dream – miles apart from the way things are. 'Yes . . . Often,' I reply softly.

Suddenly, in giant close-up, the Swiss pharmaceuticals man's face flashes up in front of me. His nose is two inches away from my nose and the flesh of his face sags downwards with the pull of gravity. He is bleating and crying.

'I sometimes feel I'm living in a fantasy world,' Anita continues. 'Guess I am . . . More so than you. The dungeon. The fucking radio show. The fake of it all. Sometimes it does my head in.'

I'm still hoping for sleep. I don't want to lead myself down into a buzzing, black, conversational hole which won't allow rest. I get down on to the floor, lie on a big cushion and close my eyes. Anita continues with her soliloquy for a while and when her rambling has almost stopped and is punctuated by long, sleepy pauses, I roll over and blow out the tall white altar candle which flickers beside me. I blow so hard that the whole thing topples over, spilling wax on to the carpet.

Who's hooking now? Is it the punter who's hooked to the hooker, to her easy uncomplicated sex? Is it the hooker who's hooked to the punter: to his easy money, to Easy Street, to his sex? Or is it that the hooker is hooked to something much more

37

than sex; she needs to be wanted, to be had, to be held, to be revered, to be abused? Call all these factors ingredients. Put them in a liquidizer and mix them up together. There you have it: prostitution.

Somewhere along the line I got hooked. I was hooked to the extent that I chose to carry on working even though, financially, there was no need. By the time I was hooked I didn't know what else to do. By then I felt that there were no other career options open. I could have lived off John, sure, but it has never been my way to live off a lover like a huge tapeworm. I'm proud of one thing: I never prostituted myself in my marriage. I never bartered sex for anything.

6

Night falls quickly, far faster than it does at home: it goes from light to dark within twenty minutes. I sit in a white wicker chair, paint peeling, paint to be picked off its legs like a scab, and rock, rock, rock. The evenings when I'm not working, I sit and watch the fruitbats swing off the gum trees, and I listen to the screech and squawk of the cockatoos and parakeets. Birdsong here sounds harsh, like a witch's cackle.

These evenings when I'm not working, or when I am working and I'm just waiting for the phone to go and I'm dolled up in black underwear, my dress hanging limp on the wardrobe door, I replay. I try to scrutinize my life so far, frame by frame.

Only days ago, when I first escaped, I tortured myself with happy memories. In off-guarded moments, I told myself I was a fool to leave. Now it is as if a kind God has pressed my subconscious survival button and the warm memories, which I was painfully clinging to, have disappeared and all I'm left with is the cold. The cold can be painful, although right now it is somehow functional; it justifies my leaving.

I have trouble remembering any soft, truly tender moments between us, any times when we were just lazy; days, weeks, months, when we fitted into each other effortlessly.

Compared to other marriages, ours was a freak; it was abnormal, an eccentric. We never trundled a lopsided trolley along smooth, anonymous supermarket corridors. We never did normal things. Even the food we ate was extreme – extremely good but never ordinary. It was the stuff that John brought home from work – cordon bleu leftovers.

Outside the Regent Hotel, the man who picked me up in the

Jaguar, when I was perched on my scrappy leather bag, to him everything was possible. His extremism, his belief that he could have it all, like a kid run riot in a toyshop, was what I fell in love with.

He faded like an old T-shirt, until at the very end he said that he had no idea what he wanted, the only thing that he knew for sure was a reverse knowledge: he knew what he didn't want and he didn't want to take responsibility for throwing in the towel.

I sleep, or – more correctly – I try to sleep, a lot. In fact, I hardly sleep at all. Although my house is quiet, hidden down a suburban backwater, with no noisy neighbours and no screaming kids, its creaks and knocks disturb me. When I come home from a job it takes me three hours to unwind and to feel still enough to sleep. When I finally do sleep the sleep comes in jolts, like short, sharp commercials. I long for one big calm sweep of sleep, one sustained eight-hour programme which plays continuously, without interruption.

I have dreams. One night I dream I am in a dark room which is cold – a sub-zero temperature. The cold hurts: it burns my limbs and my whole body feels as if it has been locked in a freezer or dangled in a freezing lake. In this extreme burning cold, whilst I'm struggling to remain conscious, someone is fucking me. I scream; he doesn't stop. He puts a hand over my face and muffles my mouth with his flat, sweaty, salty palm. His face is covered by a stocking which squashes his features; he looks android, inhuman.

A door bangs shut in the house next door and I jump awake. Relief washes through me like the first seconds of an anaesthetic. I turn on the bedside light. The dazzle disinfects; whatever demons were lurking clean disappear. I feel safe and the world, or these four walls of my bedroom, seems entirely comfortable, like an old pair of favourite shoes. I fall back to sleep.

'What do you want to drink?'

Him drinking and me not; it was always the two of us meeting on different levels, not meeting at all. It was always him trying to force stuff on me or into me or over me.

At the end, there were days spent by the poolside, him reading detective novels, always a drink beside him. If I joined him we would be two bodies occupying adjacent sun-loungers, face up to the sky, unconnected as two hard-boiled eggs in separate eggcups. At six he would get up, maybe murmur goodbye, and leave for work.

He'd come home late, after midnight. If I was working, the chances were that I would be out and we wouldn't meet until the next afternoon, and then it would be beside the pool which both of us had lost interest in dipping into.

It must have been like making love to a showroom dummy, because at the end I was never there. I was absent, looking down at my body going through the motions, working like clockwork, hovering above it. I keep coming back to that image: my own body hovering above itself. I am divided.

The punches came regularly – like drips from a tap with a cranky washer. My face, her face, would be left looking like an aubergine-topped pizza: red, yellow and puffed up with purple bruises. She stayed in the security of the blows. She stayed there with him, beside him, extracting his pleas and believing his apologies. She felt his shame and she accepted his guilt. She believed that the fury and the pitch of the fights amounted to true love.

Cut it here. I can't go on. The fact is that I waited, hoping for a sea change, too scared and lazy to give up what I knew for what I didn't. In some dumb, funny way, it suited me. Our dance was carefully choreographed and we had both written the routine. I understood the punches; I knew the steps. I take responsibility for my side of the deal.

7

Anita is impossible, but however impossible she is to be around, she's lovable and her friends forgive her. She has a golden heart. It might be cracked or misshapen, but it's large and it contains something which she gives, indiscriminately, to all. 'That's just Anita, we'll allow it.' But you wouldn't allow it with anyone else. You wouldn't brush aside the abrupt, rude phone calls, the silences in the middle of the conversations, the moods. She'll phone up and then there'll be a spitting sound and she'll be brushing her teeth whilst you're speaking to her. You'll call her at a polite hour, early evening around six and if you've woken her her reaction will be 'Fuck you and fuck off!' – not a hint of 'Don't worry, I'll get back to sleep.' Anita is Anita. As a child, she was original. As an adult, she is eccentric.

She is in love with Sydney and she loves it as if it were a drug, blurring the edges, making her forget. The heat and the blue skies clear away any mood that she might be feeling.

Soon after she arrived she bought a car with well-earned money and picked up a guy who was washing her windows at the traffic junction and drove out west, straight away, over and beyond the mountains, that same evening. They ran out of petrol. The phone went in the middle of the night. By that stage, I was back working too and I thought that it was going to be a late job which I didn't want and I wasn't going to answer. But some telepathic connection made me pick up the phone on the tenth ring, just as Anita was about to ring off. She wanted money. I told her to work out the problem herself: there was nothing I could do at that time of night short of driving out to fetch her and I was damned if I was going to do that. It ended up that the guy had a credit card anyway and they were back the next afternoon, easy as pie.

She worked three months with a smile on her face, pale pink lipstick on her lips, a business suit on her back and a pair of pearl studs in her ears. She often came round to our house and we would work from the same phone. We would get dressed and lie around in our absurd underwear and face paint and watch TV and would wait for the phone to ring. After it did, and we had both been out, we would count up the ten-dollar notes as if it was toy money, stacking little piles of it all over the floor. On good days it can feel as if the whole world is a monopoly board.

Anita soon discovered that she wasn't cut out for straight work. 'Jeez, Ruby. I can get a lot more than this . . .' She had met another girl through the agency, Linda, who had set up as a part-time S & M mistress and Anita figured that she could get a lot more money if she too began to specialize.

She called herself Sister Scourge. The Sister bit is unusual; most mistresses simply stick to the prefix 'Mistress', but Anita had to be a cut above the others, and she was. She painted her flat an even darker shade of purple and commissioned some poor boy who she met in the park, whilst he was innocently flying his kite and walking his dog, to build some stocks. She bought some whips and reins from a riding stables that was closing down and she was off and away.

Initially, I was concerned for her. There are nutters out there and I didn't think that she fully understood the vulnerability of her position. She understood the theatre and the rhetoric (she had read the books) but that was all. She tried to allay my fears. First, she would only do dominatrix work, therefore she was hardly vulnerable. Secondly, her clients were to be vetted at source, the source being the agency. She went in to see Barry one night after nine when he had had a few drinks and had struck an easy deal with him: a twenty-eighty cut rather than a forty-sixty one.

She also says that 90 per cent of her clients are regular and if they're not, and Barry doesn't know of them, then all she has to

43

do is phone up one of the other mistresses for a low-down. Chances are that someone would have heard of him.

Finally she went to the stray dogs' home and rescued a creature from Death Row. He was an enormous Alsatian dog – a wolf-like animal – who she called Wayne. He looks evil but he is a good-hearted beast, soft as toasted marshmallow. When she's working she puts a muzzle over his sloppy nose, ties his leather lead to the bedpost and cranks up his frustration levels so that all – she informs her quivering, submissive clients as soon as they've walked in that door – she would have to do if things got out of hand would be to unleash him and scream 'GO, BOY, GO!' and Wayne would leap on the bed, gnashing his pointed, canine teeth at the man's neck. 'Nah . . . I'm safe,' she kept saying.

And then the phone-in show had come up, like everything does in her life, without her really having to try, like golden brown toast popping up from a toaster, effortlessly. A DJ friend of hers, Jackie, was working for the station and, when the job had come free, had told the boss that she knew a woman who would rise to a challenge and who could speak sugar sex sense. The boss (big glasses, desk-bound) took Jackie's streetwise words as the ultimate wisdom. Anita was offered the job blind.

An hour before the first show she had got the jitters. 'I can't do it, Rue . . . How can I . . . me?'

Positivity was the only trump card. 'You can,' I kept saying, trying to convince both myself and her that she might be able to pull it off. 'You can!' And she did. Within four months she became cult listening. People stayed in to listen to her.

One afternoon, about six months ago, I was driving through the Cross and I saw her wandering along the pavement. She was wearing one of her many wigs and I had to look twice to check it was her – not only because of her suddenly tousled blonde mane but also because of the way she was walking, her gait. She was meandering. She was due on air in three hours.

'That figures,' John had said, lucidly, when I told him about Anita drifting through the Cross. It was as if he knew something about her that I didn't. 'That figures,' he repeated.

A couple of months later, she was at the sink, ploughing her way through a week's washing-up and I had handed her a dirty mug. A syringe was slopping about in the dregs.

One evening, it must be about five thirty, since the young-suited yuppie from the house opposite has just got home from work and has stepped out on to his balcony to shoo away a ginger tom-cat, I am sitting on the veranda when the phone rings. It's Anita. Her tone sounds anxious. 'Can I come round?'

I had been counting on some quiet time to myself but I have a problem saying 'No'. 'Yes,' I reply.

Crash: she drops the receiver on the floor before managing to hang up.

I walk on to the road and look up it in the direction that she will be coming from. We have been having sporadic rain lately, and it begins to rain now, at first slowly and within minutes so hard that the raindrops are the size of pear drops and fall from the sky like heavy lead pellets. They hit and bounce off the tin roofs and splat over the tarmac road and the waxy leaves of the shrubs. I stand in this warm rain for a minute or two, letting it soak me. As I'm going back indoors, a cab pulls up, swishing the water in the gutter, and Anita, bedraggled and thinner than ever, clambers out, fidgets around with a purse and hands the change through the driver's open window. When the transaction is com-plete, she walks up the steps and, without greeting me, says simply, 'This came.'

She produces, from the cuff of her zebra-skin-lapelled cowboy boot, a piece of pink paper.

'Know anything about it?'

I immediately recognize John's handwriting. It is a calligraphic style: manicured, precise, utterly meticulous and contrived. I unfold the paper and read the words: 'Watching you. Watch out.'

'You've not heard from him?'

'No.'

'Well, I can fucking do without it, Rue. Tell him to fucking get his shit together. I don't need little creeps like him buzzing around

45

me like mozzies. "Watching you. Watch out." For God's sake – couldn't he have thought up something more adventurous?'

Two days later, a second note arrives, this one addressed to me. Like the first note, it is written on pink notepaper and contains exactly the same message. It is pushed under my front door late one night. This means John has found out where I am living. I am scared.

Just an 'Oh' when I tell Anita, by phone, about the further development. She might be mid-session, because she answers breathlessly. 'Can't talk now,' she says. 'Speak later.'

I call up work and tell them to put me on call all day and all night. 'Hang on, darling,' the smooth secretary purrs. She has been hired because her voice will pull in punters. 'Baz wants a word.' I rehearse my 'I don't fuck with the boss' line in my head.

In fact Barry isn't going to offer me either his money or his dick; he is about to offer me a job that is to be a grand beginning. 'Ruby?' His intonation rises with the last syllable. He speaks with that old Aussie twang which makes everything sound like a question and which gives the sense that the entire nation is built on insecurity. It is early morning, a good time for Barry since he is sober, or hung over, and less offensive than usual.

'How kinky do you go?'

I reply tamely to a tame question.

'Weak-tea kinky. I leave the hard stuff to the specialists.'

An acquaintance of his, who won't give his name, wants some lukewarm fantasy work doing, nothing heavy. He will pay way over the odds and the job's an overnight one. Baz thinks I'm the woman. I'm built right, I curve and bend in the right places, and more to it, hearsay has it, I have the 'right head'.

'Less of the sweet talk, Baz. Tell me who else has seen him.' I will cover myself and do some research before committing.

'Hang about.' He puts down the phone and, after a few seconds, returns with the booking diary. 'Charlotte. Helen.'

Charlotte is one of the few black women working at the agency and she's cool. She works for an HIV charity and through her

46

charity work we all get the rubbers for free, which is a bigger gift than the government will hand out.

Like Anita, Charlotte sounds as if she is fresh out of bed, caught on a job. She remembers the man well.

'He's cool . . . Nothing heavy. Do it. I would. Fuck it that he didn't ask for me again. What the hell did I do wrong? Probably didn't suck enough. He was big on sucking, arsehole. Yeah, he tips well. Yeah, I remember the tips. Oh, do it. It's easy. Been busy?'

'Not really . . . You?'

'Nah. What with the airport strike and the recession. Not much at all.'

Punters always want to fuck. Dicks always get hard. They say that wives say no and never understand them. All of this happens recession or no recession, and our clients are hardly the type worst hit by the falling dollar. Any worker knows that; I'm surprised that Charlotte has bought into Baz's boring, recognizable smooth talk.

We pass more time-of-day pitter-patter. We bitch about the receptionists at VIP, gossip about Baz's private life and the exotic young woman who has recently been drifting around his office in designer labels calling the slug 'Darling'. Finally we call it a day and hang up.

I call Barry back, accept the job and scribble down details of time and place.

Later that evening I take the elevator and go up to room 666 and I do the condom meditation outside the room's glossy green-painted door. A white rubber is pulled down over my head, rolled tight over my body. None of myself can flow out and none of the client will be able to seep inside me. From the other side of the door I hear the sound of loud opera. This must be music for perverts – Anita is often playing the same tunes. It's from *The Magic Flute* – a bold sound. I lift my hand up to knock on the door but it opens before my knuckles have time to rap. He must have been looking through the peephole.

He is maybe thirty-six, thirty-seven at the most, and he is tall and dark and he has brown eyes. He looks regular, or a bit better than regular. He looks like Superman or Action Man. My initial thoughts are 'boring'. My initial thoughts, as he stands at the door, sizing me up, are 'in out in out in out, over in a shot'. This is the type of guy who works hard as a lawyer all day and then works out in the gym with the boys and talks to them about sport or even the sport he played at college ten years ago.

'Your real name Ruby?'

'Yes.'

He stands back and lets me walk into the corridor of his plush suite.

'I believe you,' he says.

I don't give a shit whether he believes me or not but I'm angry at his arrogance in even suspecting that I might. Of course, I'm smart enough not to let my anger show. At this early, nascent stage it wouldn't help. I'm here now and I'm here to please and here to walk out rich. I keep my Barbie Doll smile stuck on my face and I think dollars.

Suddenly he grabs hold of the straps of my handbag, which is slung diagonally across my breasts, and he tugs the straps ferociously. I tumble from the corridor into the doorway of the white-tiled bathroom. I eye up the freebies: the shampoos and soaps and the towels and bathrobes. Nothing catches my eye, there's nothing new to rip off. Back home I have enough soap to wash me clean for a lifetime. Then I notice the toilet paper. It comes with pale-green oak leaves inked into it. I decide to help myself to a roll later on.

'Come here!'

'I already am.'

This guy really is a headfucker. I suspect that he wants to be someone he's not. He is pretending to be rich and famous when he is most likely a computer salesman from hicksville.

'Sure,' I reply, pandering a little more, thinking tips and thinking specifically of a dress I saw earlier in the day in a boutique on Glebe Point Road. It's always best to make the dicks feel important. I've learnt how to go straight for the ego, massage it, and fan it as if it were the dying embers of a fire. Then it will flush into flame.

He looks me straight in the eyes. I feel violated, raped by his vision, which is just the way he wants it to be. I turn my head, look just off-centre, over his bulky shoulder. I study the grouting between the white tiles. I check his hands for weapons. They are empty; there's no gun.

He kicks the door of the bathroom shut. It automatically locks behind him. The towel which was wrapped around his waist falls to the ground. He's hard. I study his penis, weigh it up for aesthetics and for signs of disease. There is none. I do this to all dicks – give them marks out of ten. This one is straight and thick and smooth and long and something inside me clicks.

I move close to him, begin to kiss his face and the smooth skin of his neck, just beneath the shaving line. He tears off my clothes until they lie in a pool around my feet and then he bangs off the bathroom light so that the windowless room is pitch black. We fuck in the dark, standing up, my legs wrapped round his waist.

When it is over he kicks open the door. A slant of light shines in. 'Come through,' he says, and I follow.

'Money,' he says when we get to the main room. He opens a bedside drawer and pulls out four grand cash and tosses me the bundle. I count it methodically and shove it into my shoe. I climb on to the bed. I don't want to talk. I reach for the TV remote control and switch it on. He doesn't want any hooker pussyfooting chitchat either, no 'Where you from?' or 'Have you used Barry before?' He's beyond niceties. 'I'm going down for dinner. You stay here. Order anything you want up.'

As soon as he is gone, I ring up room service and order a pineapple and some bananas and some grapes. 'Your needs are modest,' he remarks when he returns. 'That's all you want?' I nod.

'Good meal?' I ask him, then wish I could retract the question since it seems too personal and somehow, in this setting, inappropriate. He nods. 'So so.'

He rings the changes. His tongue moves down my body,

49

between my breasts, over my stomach, encircling my belly button, down in a straight line until it reaches my cunt. He licks and sucks with tenderness and compassion, and then he switches mood and fucks so hard that I bruise inside.

'Shit!' I say when it's over, and I'm recovering my breath and it's four a.m. and the first one-legged pigeons are beginning to purr on the window-ledge outside. Despite the bruises, for one of the first times ever on a job, I come out smiling. This isn't meant to happen. I'm scared. I think I'm falling into something and I don't quite know, or like, what it is.

I leave before breakfast. I arrived at eight the previous night, so theoretically I can leave before eight this morning. If I go whilst he is still wanting more, he'll ask for me again. He tips me the biggest tip I have ever received.

He comes running after me, down the quiet and muffled hotel corridor, which tinkles with faraway tea trolleys and chambermaids doing their jobs.

'Have this!'

He hands me a thick navy cashmere winter overcoat although it is a balmy, still autumn day outside.

'It'll mean I have to come back . . . I want to fuck you some more. Do some stuff with you.'

I suddenly remember that Barry had mentioned the fantasy work. Somehow, in the heat of the night, I had forgotten all about it.

'Sure,' I go, puzzled over this coat stuff. It's a nice coat, worth a bob or two. 'Sure,' I repeat. Then I add professionally, 'Call me via Barry,' and I waddle off up the corridor, too sore to stride.

When I'm back home, Anita phones again.

'Done anything about the note?'

I'm only just in and I'm lying heavy-limbed, soup-limbed, muddy-limbed, on the sofa.

'No.'

'Do it . . . It'll get worse. I know him. I know his moves.'

'He's *my* husband,' I reply. I know him better than she does. Tit for tat, I behave like a child.

'Call him. Get in touch with him and tell him to stop it.'
'When I'm ready to,' I go. 'Now I need to sleep.'
'OK . . . OK . . . OK . . .'

PART TWO

8

'The money holds the sex in place, John. The money makes the sex possible. The only kind of sex that's free is the one you pay for.'

'Without the money, you wouldn't do it with any one of them?'
'No.'

I would spend hours explaining how it was with my clients, saying that however many of them there were, I was always faithful to him because he was the only one I made love to. He would hear me and, I think, believe me. Or, he would hold on to what I said about faith and betrayal until the moment that I left for another job and then he would lose his own faith and he would sink back into the old fears – that he wasn't good enough. The old insecurities would reappear.

I was telling the truth. There wasn't one single client who I'd have done it with for any other reason than money. I hired out my body and I gave him my soul. I can't afford to believe that it was the other way round. It was not.

He answers on the first ring. My heart jumps and lodges in my throat like a golfball.

'John?'

Silence. Since he answered so fast, he must be in bed, right beside the phone. The big windows will be open and the splendid king-size bed will dominate the room, its white counterpane dimpled like fields.

'What's the note about?'

Despite my beating heart, I speak evenly. 'Can we meet?' I ask. It is unlike him to be so reticent in replying. He must have someone there with him, lying beside him. I have interrupted something. A perfect woman and a perfect love has formed miraculously, risen up out of nowhere like a perfect soufflé, within the course of a month. I try to fight off what my sane mind knows is most likely fiction.

'John? You there?'

'Sure.'

He replies very calmly, detached, like a shrink might talk to a client. Our roles seem reversed: suddenly I am the lunatic and John is the still point.

'Sure we can meet up,' he says after a long pause which hangs expectantly in the air like a break between radio shows. 'Sure we can meet up,' and he suggests a time and a place.

'Deal.'

She must have long white fingers. Her smooth hands slide between his thighs. She must have big soft cushion-like lips, naturally reddened, lips to die for. I pull myself back into the present, into what I know is real. A horrid bird perches on a horrid twig on the brown glaze of a garage giveaway mug.

'See you tomorrow then,' I say.

'Bye.'

As soon as I have put down the receiver, the phone rings again. This time it's Barry, speaking in a silky voice, fake come-on, fake something, maybe just plain fake. The gentleman was impressed. He wants me again, tonight, 'Toute suite, pronto.' Barry is a Euro snob. He has always coveted Europeanisms.

I'm too tired to work. I wouldn't be able to pull it off. Barry comes out with a well-rehearsed spiel, the one that Charlotte gave me the night before: I'm a lucky woman, I should be thankful for any job, especially given Australia's collapsed economic climate.

If I lose the job, I lose it. I hold my ground. Once I do so he accepts it. 'OK, lady, OK.'

Ten minutes later the phone rings again. I get what I want. The man will wait. We will meet again on Thursday at the same place, at the same time.

I replay moments from the night before. I remember his arms, from the elbow up – the smooth dark-brown skin, the gentle bulge of the muscles below, the veins trickling over his skin like the ink wiggles of roads on a map. I turn soft inside, like a slowly ripening banana. I'm sleepy and mushy. I jump awake. Those are forbidden feelings. First rule this: he is a client, a John, an anonymous man. Obsessions are not allowed.

I spend the night twitching, hardly sleeping at all. At dawn I get up and walk to the pool. I need a purification process before my appointment. I do twenty laps, chug up and down like a wind-up boat, and when I clamber out of the pool, I feel still and settled like a millpond.

The café is on the third floor and it hangs over a tiered, Victorian arcade, its tables and chairs spreading out over a spacious, iron-balustraded balcony. I take a seat by the railings and look down through three storeys on to the arcade below. This is a ritzy cul-de-sac of town, an enclave amongst the tack of the high-street shops outside. There aren't many people in the café: a few women who are taking coffee in pairs, gossiping, brandishing designer shopping bags and talking divorce lawyers and settlements.

I see John coming. He strides out confidently over the black-and-white chessboard tiles of the ground floor. He bobs into the mahogany-veneered lift and within two minutes he is at my table, swinging back the chair, flopping into it and smoothly whipping out a packet of mild cigarettes from his denim shirt pocket. He lights up. All of this is accomplished without either a kiss, a hello or a greeting.

'So what's the problem?'

I take the pink letter out of my bag and hand it over to him.

'This.'

He roughly takes hold of the envelope, smirks and tosses it back over the table-top. A waitress with a thick German accent comes over to deliver my coffee and take John's mineral water order.

'Don't have an answer,' he says as soon as she is gone.

'Well fucking stop it,' I snap.

He smirks, then eyeballs me. Although I am determined to win the psychic match, I don't manage to stay the course. Looking into his eyes is too difficult, too threatening. 'Why?' I ask, looking back at the envelope. 'You can't justify it, can you?'

He shrugs his shoulders nonchalantly. 'Don't have to. Do I? . . . If we're on to "whys?" Why do you keep doing it? Answer me that, darling! Why are you so fucking easy?'

I don't reply.

'Yeah, *you* can't justify it either, can you?'

'I don't bloody have to,' I snarl.

'You better get moving. Better get off your back and into a solicitor's office. Or back on to your back. Maybe one of your clients could do the work for you. Save you a grand or two. Let's hurry through this parting, honey. Let's kill it – eh?'

'Fuck off, John. Fuck right off.'

'Tell that slut Anita she's gonna get it too. Tell her to go fuck herself. Tell her to straighten up too.'

He begins to cry. At first there's a sniffle and then a sob and then he is really crying making a noise so loud that the couple on the next table turn round and stare. I remain stone-cold silent. I don't want to touch him – I don't want any connection at all. At the same time I feel as if I should be reaching out, being that mother, holding him in my arms, comforting. I stick out the silence and watch him cry. I chop and turn inside.

Finally I get up, put two bucks down on the table and leave without a goodbye. Outside on the street, my heart is racing. I scrounge a fag from a woman standing at the bus stop, flowery skirt, dyed red hair, in her fifties, and curse myself for doing so. I gave up smoking two years back. I'm shaking.

Replay. Sometimes I can't switch off this replay button. At night, we were in bed, the lights were out. The telephone rang. We were in each others' arms. Dring dring. Dring dring. Up I got, rolled on my stockings, lashed on that lipstick, went out to a job. John would be left in the dark with only his right hand to comfort him. That's when I felt guilty.

Guilt lingers like a virus. How do I drop it? Letting it go must be somehow connected with forgiveness, with giving something to somebody. What is required is for me to give something to myself; I can't imagine doing that.

'I'll be back,' I would say, bending over him, kissing his face and putting my tongue in his ear, sliding it down over his neck, sliding it down, down, down over his jungle chest, circumnavigating the thick, semi-matted curly silver-grey whorls of hair. 'Wait for me – all right?'

Two hours later, I'd be back. I'd tiptoe in, afraid of waking him. I'd creep into the bathroom and take off all the make-up and I'd always shower, shower until I was squeaky virgin clean. Then I would get into bed. 'I've waited for you,' I would whisper. I had done. I always waited.

I remember Palm Beach, Christmas time, midsummer. It was soon after the Harbourside restaurant had opened and John was becoming known as a restaurateur with flair. That time was good. If there was a high point between us it would have been those three summer months.

John had looks and he had style and he had English charm. Young, keen Sydney-sider female journalists thought he was a darling. I found that bit hard; I was jealous of the foodie bimbos – the Pollys, Natashas, Suzannes, Joannas and Lydias – who would come over and interview him, always perfectly turned out, in linen jackets and linen suits, asking his opinion on nouvelle cuisine. I bit my lip every time one showed up at the house, Filofax and tape-recorders in hand. I tried to be cool, but I was anything but cool inside. I'd go indoors and play loud music. I would drown anything I was feeling out with music. John had his drink; I had my music. He drank his troubles away and I blasted mine out, or tried to. He didn't do anything with any of these girls; he would even laugh about them after they had left, joke at their fluttering eyelids, joke at the flirts, joke about the messages they would leave on the answering machine, messages where an allure wavered and dangled in between the pauses and the sighs and the tones, in the spaces between words.

Christmas, that was good. We had a party to celebrate the

wharf opening. We hired a house out on Palm Beach for the summer, invited 200 people over one Sunday lunch, and the party sprawled out, through the house, over the gardens and down on to the beach. By mid-afternoon, we snuck away like teenagers, almost guiltily. We went down to the ocean and scrambled over the clump of rocks at the far end of the bay and found a patch of firm, hard sand.

At the end, if we did it at all, we fucked. Or hardly that, which implies some degree of intensity: we glided in and out of each other coolly, mechanically, like glycerined machinery. During those summer months, it was different. Nothing, either inside us or outside us, seemed to be putting up a resistance. Everything was easy. We had something; it felt strong and indestructible and it glistened, like shining stainless-steel knife blades. I remember strolling back along the beach, towards the house, toes digging into the wet sand, clutching it between strides. It was turning dark and music from the house caught in the wind and wafted along the beach in gusts. 'I'll be frank,' John had said in an overblown way. 'I don't understand women . . . All I know is this: that they are usually smaller than I am, they have soft skin and they bleed once a month.' I miss his humour. I miss his finely delivered wit. He had grabbed me, hugged me, kissed me. 'I love you, Rue. I really do.' I held him and gave him the longest kiss ever.

I felt taken care of. I felt someone durable and solid was really there, right next to me, like a rock with a heart. What I wanted, what I tried to see, was a man of living granite. I wanted something to tether myself to, to ground myself in, be anchored by.

And still I worked. I needed to. If I hadn't I would have become wholly reliant on him. I would have become a decoration, a gilded bauble hanging off the branch of a Christmas tree. The worse things got between us, the more jobs I would take. Like mine, John's work also became an escape clause, a panic button which he pressed when he was in trouble.

9

'Who are you?' There is no reply. He just won't say. 'Who are you?' I giggle this time. Maybe that will goad it out of him, wheedle it out like a splinter from the thick skin of a heel. Oh, I know all the tricks, all the ploys, a giggle here, an eye roll there, a sigh, a pause, a wink, an act, a mattress act. Lastly I shout, *'Who are you?'* I yell. I scream.

He still won't give his name. His namelessness is beginning to bug me. I'm no naïve rose-petal *ingenue* who has fallen into the game and doesn't understand the exact rules. I'll not blubber and commit *faux pas*. My lips are sealed. I'll not ring up the tabloids. I respect my clients' demand for confidentiality but I expect a measure of openness in return. I feel as if he doesn't trust my professionalism.

We are in the same hotel room as before. This time the forest-green curtains are drawn open and the room, I now see, overlooks the harbour. It is a bright sunny late afternoon and the crescent-shaped harbour bridge smiles brilliantly, like a new moon.

'Don't you ever watch TV?' he asks in reply to my 'Who are you?'

'No.'

We fuck a second time, watch some TV, raid the minibar and fuck a third time. In between the sex there's no conversation, just TV news coverage. Although I'm still angry at the anonymity, there is something about this man linked to his broad, easy grin when he opens the door for me which dissipates my anger. Afterwards, when I'm lying back in the feather pillows, with a G & T beside me and he is making some phone calls, *sotto voce*, in the next-door room, I feel that I'm glowing, like the hands of a luminous alarm clock in the dark.

The next morning I leave at ten. He has a business meeting in town. His driver drops me off home before taking him on to Martin Place. The car is a navy-blue Daimler. The driver is a small fellow, American, who covers his bald pate with a peaked prep school cap. I am delivered like a pizza to my front door: I feel like a princess.

I spend the rest of the morning loafing. Whole hours float by like balloons.

Later that afternoon, I go round to Anita's. When there is no reply and I have turned my back on her glossed black door and am half-way down the smelly damp staircase, she answers with a grudging, 'Hi.'

'Am I interrupting anything?'

'Not exactly. No . . . Come in.'

Her tiny body is shrouded by an enormous Mickey Mouse T-shirt, beneath which pops out a polka-dot red and white skirt. The shirt is off-beat Hollywood – offbeat in that Mickey and Minnie are going at each other hammer and tongs, fighting like cat and dog.

She leads me down the artery – a narrow, dark-purple-painted corridor – into the heart of the house. Here, in the living room, the thin white tracing-paper blinds are pulled down so that the bright sunlight is diffused and the air is blue with cigarette smoke. Sitting on the long sofa is Sam, the guy Anita used to live with until a year or so ago. I'm surprised to see him since when they split it had been messy and I didn't know they were still in touch. Sam has always been the type who's too cool to say hello. Today he just about manages a nod and pretty much immediately stands up, mumbling something about having to make a move.

'You well?' I ask him. Anita is crouched down over the record collection, fumbling for some music. He has just moved studios and for the first time in his career as a furniture designer-cum-dealer, the designing, rather than the other, is paying the bills. He is selling well. 'Got a job from John,' he says.

A year ago John had asked for Sam's number. At the time I gave it him because I thought that any vague success that Sam might enjoy, might make things easier between Anita and him. The restaurant in Melbourne needed some new tables, things shaped like kidney beans, and Sam was the man. At least it was a move up from making dominatrix's racks and medieval beds.

He moves over to Anita, kisses the nape of her neck. Simultaneously, at the wrong volume, music crashes into the room through two giant matt-black speakers which are hanging at odd angles, off the wall. Anita ignores him. She doesn't move in response to his kiss and he walks out, carefree.

The Chubb on the front door clicks shut and Anita pulls herself up from the floor and into an armchair.

During her disentanglement from Sam she kept all her feelings to herself and she remained silent to the end. As far as I know, she spoke to no one about what was going on and the only sign that things were awry was her spectacular weight loss and the common knowledge that Sam was man about town, loafing around, in and out of everyone's bed. Sam had hurt her, though she would never profess hurt. Instead she kept silent and channelled her hurt and anger into expanding her Sister Scourge client list.

'You OK?' I ask. I figure that a simple question like that isn't intrusive.

'Sure.'

She reaches for her cigarettes, breaks a match trying to light one, strikes another, hits the jackpot and inhales deeply.

'Heard from the prick?'

'Don't call him that.'

'Sorry. "John." Heard from the "John" then?'

Part of me still wants to defend John, to protect him. At best Anita's tongue is sharp and today, post whatever happened with Sam, it will most likely be serrated. She continues.

'Someone's been calling the station. Leaving threatening messages. Think it's him?'

I avoid the question, tell her instead about the meeting, and

63

about John's quirky, erratic behaviour. I leave out his closing lines. They have haunted me; I keep remembering the words about telling Anita she's going to get it. She listens half-heartedly and after I've come to a close lashes out again.

'Think it's him? I was asking about the phone calls to the station. Think it's him or are you gonna ignore my question?'

'Possibly.'

'Possibly what? Possibly it's him or possibly you'll ignore my question?'

'Possibly both.'

She raises her eyes. A girl's voice chimes out of the speakers. She sings in high soprano – a sentimental song about farmsteads and fields and roads and white-lace dresses. I lean back into the cushions and close my eyes, but Anita won't let me relax. She is in a mood to fight, needle and wound.

'I tried calling last night. Where were you?'

'Working,' I reply drowsily, hoping that she will let me get away with being cryptic and abstract and doubting that she will. She doesn't.

'All night? Who the hell is he?'

'Pass.'

'Who?' She cocks an eyebrow, smiling with her eyebrows rather than her lips. For a moment she looks like she did at fifteen, quizzing a school friend about a date. By now I'm getting irritated with her. She crashes through my desire for privacy with a barrage of questions.

'A client.'

She lifts both eyebrows, this time judgementally, gets up and shuffles through to the kitchen. Wayne bounds out and bounces into the living room, skidding on the rugs. I remain still as a statue, hoping that he might not notice me and hoping that his pink, dripping, wet nose will stay away. Anita returns with two chipped mugs of weak tea. 'So,' she says, crashing them down on the coffee table.

I change the topic. 'Getting much work?'

'Two jobs yesterday. Another at four today.'

She checks her watch. It's a quarter to four.

She jumps up, looks at her pale face in the mirror, pulls an ugly expression and shoos the snuffling Wayne away. She picks up a dirty make-up bag and begins a transformation process, courtesy of cheap foundation, cheap eyeliner and cheap lipstick.

'Want to meet up later? Go to the movies? I need to get out. I've stayed in for forty-eight hours. I've got cabin fever,' she says.

Finally, after an argument over whether or not to see a weepie or a comedy, we agree on mutual territory – a horror film. The film is a bold American movie, chock-a-block with teenagers wearing blue jeans and pastel shirts which are the colours of sugared almonds. The kids usually get attacked whilst bicycling around quiet, leafy suburbia in the twilight hours. We take seats in the back row and snicker through most of it.

I shut my eyes and eliminate the corny visuals. I make up a movie in my head which fits the soundtrack's pants, sighs, screams, beatings. My movie is scary whilst the one on screen is not. I am numb to visuals.

When the movie is over and we are standing on George Street, with the rain tumbling down and arms stuck out at right angles to hail a cab, Anita says, 'There's something I want to say.'

I am licking a green cone of pistachio ice-cream and I reply whilst I'm struggling with one hand on the ice and the other on an intransigent umbrella.

At that point, when she is drawing a huge breath which suggests she needs a lot of oxygen to get through an imminent disclosure, a taxi with a VACANT sign rolls into sight. My umbrella shoots up and unfolds like a blackbird shaking its wings in a bird-bath. The taxi stops, splashing water on to the pavement, missing our legs by a few inches. A tall man rushes out from the cinema's foyer, where he has been sheltering from the downpour. He tries to grab the taxi but our swift actions – car door open, address delivered to the driver, icy 'Excuse me' delivered expertly, with authority and cold anger – have him scurrying back to cover. His face looks familiar. 'D'you recognize him?' I ask Anita, who is half inside the cab. She shakes her head. 'Nah.' The struggle for the cab makes the moment lost for whatever it was that was about to be said. The cab pulls off. I cross the road and go off in the other direction home.

Back home, I turn out the lights, clamber into bed, snuggle down under the duvet and listen to the radio.

He comes on third, after a series of pretty routine questions about hysterectomies and condoms. 'We have a Mr Hart from Point Piper on the line. Go ahead, Mr Hart.' My muscles tighten up; they feel brittle like burnt plastic.

'Hello,' she goes. 'What's your question?'

She must know exactly who it is, yet she remains impeccably professional and anonymous.

'Is that Anita Schwartz?'

'Yes.'

'I don't have a question. I have something I'd like your opinion on, though.'

'Yes,' she says slowly, as if she's falling into treacle and she can't pull herself out.

'I know who you are. You're not Anita Schwartz. You're Sister Scourge. You're a sham woman. You're a fucking sham. One big lie. I'd like to make you suffer. Make you squirm. Put you in pain. Make you bleed sister, mistress, madam . . .'

He pauses, draws breath and then recommences, this time with gusto.

'Listeners, go visit Sydney's leading mistress: Sister Scourge. Telephone 02 358 7878. Phone for a session now!'

'I'm afraid we'll have to cut you off there,' she says icily.

'Watch it. Just fucking watch it.'

His voice trails off. The line goes bleep and then a long chunk of commercials comes on and a woman chats to a next-door neighbour over a garden fence about biological soap powder and about washing shirts.

I switch off the radio. My telephone rings. I pick it up. 'Hello?' I say, but I'm speaking into a silence; no one replies or responds.

'Hello,' I go again.

The line buzzes dead.

Without thinking too much about it, I hang up. Immediately it rings again.

'Slut!'

I hang up. It was John's voice.

The phone rings once more. This time I disconnect, get up and check that the doors are locked firm.

10

As we parted last time, in the sweet-smelling leather-seated back of the blue Daimler, conversation overheard by the earflapping chauffeur, he asked for my number. I gave it him.

I wouldn't usually do this, have never done it before, but it felt safe. At first I was uncertain about bypassing Barry. If he feels he is being cheated, he could do a fetching number in demanding free favours. But then this man so rarely uses the agency that Barry won't miss his custom, or suspect foul play. I agree.

He's due round today. He will call before he arrives and therefore, it follows, I have to reconnect the phone. I do so gingerly.

As soon as I do it rings.

'Fucking slut.'

'*Fuck off!*' I scream.

'Get fucking ready . . . Whore . . . Sack . . . Jug . . . Receptacle.'

It's John. He speaks very slowly and deliberately, pausing in between each word.

For emergencies, an old tin whistle dangles beside the phone. I pick it up and blow very long and very loud into the mouthpiece.

It sends them deaf. By this stage I've lost sense of who it actually is that I'm rendering deaf. It might be John; it might be anyone. I hope this dwork is going deaf. I hope he is wincing in pain, crumpling up like paper thrown on a fire, turning black, disintegrating. I hope he's rendered deaf for ever and ever. I fill my lungs with air and blow and blow and blow. It is only when I'm gulping for a fresh lungful of air that I realize the phone is humming to itself.

See me, I want to say to them all as they grind away on top of me, one the same as the next, grubby dollar notes clenched in sweaty palms or grubby dollar notes sheathed in crocodile-skin wallets. See me; see who I am.

I dream of blue sea. I'm swimming away through lukewarm water and, as I swim, I leave a trail of purple liquid, a stain which curls and twists through the water like squid's ink.

I dream too that I'm in a walled English garden. On the outside of the stoned tall wall is soft green English pastureland, a church spire, bells ringing. Inside is the most perfect garden imaginable. Here there are sweet-smelling pink tea roses and tall hollyhocks and purple rhododendrons and yellow sunflowers and blue blue delphiniums and red poppies and silvery-leafed rabbit's ears.

I cut to a client with short hairy legs and a furry back. He is pumping away on top of me, calling me names, speaking a language that I don't understand, biting my breasts until they are sore, taking snipes at my swollen nipples. I float back to the green lawn of the garden. I lie face heavenwards, looking up through a black lacework of branches. The grass sticks to my back, leaving patterns on my skin.

The phone rings shrill. I pick it up warily and when it's his voice, I relax. He is phoning with a time and a place; my flat, my territory, my land, my castle at three p.m.

'You're OK?' he asks, picking up on my nervousness.

'Yes,' I reply drowsily. 'Yes' comes naturally to me. It's a knee-jerk reaction like 'Please', a legacy of white knee-socks, of being told to watch my Ps and Qs. It is also a legacy of working.

'Sure?'

With this man I resolve to be honest. With John I wasn't exactly dishonest, I was just silent concerning large parts of the truth. Part of the pact I now make with myself is to be honest. I'm not all right so I tell him.

'No,' I reply.

He takes another step forward.

'Anything I can do?' he asks.

69

Honesty is one step; being ready to accept help, which is part of trusting, is the next. Trust is any hooker's pitfall. It is the core of her lost innocence. I'd like to restore my ability to trust but to do so I am aware that I have to move back through the years, back to when I was a child.

As for his offer of help, for now I turn it down.

'No,' I go. 'And thanks . . .'

Come midday it's safe to call Anita. She'll be coming round from sleep. However, I don't need to pick up the phone because she turns up unannounced, leaping like an elf, or a cartoon character, over my brushwood fence and arriving, in a jump, or a swish of a magic wand, on my patio. She raps at the windows. Handsome Wayne is with her, trailing four steps behind, trained to the nth degree, on the end of a fat, thick leather leash. We go through to the kitchen. Wayne stays outdoors in the shade of the veranda, sipping water from a stainless-steel bowl as daintily as a dog can.

'Did you hear it?'

I nod.

She begins to race with her words, hardly giving me time to speak in between pauses.

'I want to call the police in . . . I want to involve them . . . He's not going to stop at a threat, Ruby.'

She unwraps a large chocolate flake. I crack an egg into the frying pan. When it meets hot fat, it sizzles.

'He's nuts. Bonkers. Caput. Ruby, he's crazy. Fucking bananas.'

She sucks on the long chocolate tube. I watch the frilly edge of the egg white turn brown.

'You deaf, Rue?'

'No. I need time to think.'

'Why?'

'I don't want to be pushed into anything. I need time to weigh things up, make the right decision.'

'Jeez . . . Fuck it, Rue. We'll leave it and wait for the consequences. Is that it? Why? Why wait?'

70

She knows exactly why. If you're a hooker, police protection or involvement is the last thing you want. Once a cop scratches your back, he wants you to scratch his. Once you've got something on him, he is a scared and therefore a potentially dangerous man. The wisest thing is to keep away from the cops for as long as you can. I think of Shirley Brifman or Sally Huxted – the list is endless of women who have fallen out with the cops and have subsequently been done in by them. I've always managed to keep out of the cops' way and I'm not sure I want to change the record now. Bolshily she agrees to my request for a day's grace. 'I guess I'll just have to go with that.'

'What were you going to tell me last night?'

She twitches and looks at the window. 'Not now . . . Later . . . Now's not good.'

'What was the reaction at the station?' I ask. 'You going to lose your job?'

'Jeez, no. No one said a word. They're either too fucking scared and they don't want to know the truth as to who I am coz they'll have to sack me and things could get nasty, or the boss was asleep and didn't hear it.'

'Nothing from the press?'

She shakes her head. This time, the entire incident has slipped through the net unnoticed.

Soon after Anita has left, he shows up punctually, to the exact minute. He wants to talk business, so I lead him through to the dining-room table. It's the first time that he has been here and he murmurs approvingly as we move through the house.

He wants to see me regularly. He wants to have access to me two days a week or one night. If it is a night, the hours will be eight to eight. If it's a day, then anything up to seven hours at a stretch. There are three options to payment. One, he offers cash at triple the normal rate. Two, he'll pay in kind. Three, he'll pay one week in kind and one week in cash.

I settle for the latter option.

The ground rules are now fixed.

Oh, I relate all of this as if it is a business arrangement, nothing more, but you can surely sniff, even if you have a peg clipped tight over your nostrils, that there's more to it than pounds, shillings and pence, and if you are extra-super, gossamer-silk sensitive, you might also sniff how duplicitous I am about feeling so excited.

I've said before, this is not allowed. I am stepping into forbidden territory – vaulting across the safety walls which divide prostitute from client. Inside the walls is a grey, indeterminate area in which neither party knows their roles and in which the definitions 'prostitute' and 'client' no longer apply.

Danger, or the hint of it, keeps me on my toes. This liaison might be dangerous. I hope there's more to it, though, than a quasi-addiction to adrenalin.

This afternoon, a hot autumn afternoon, he stays till six. It's so hot in my front room and so hot in my bedroom, everything seems so hot. At the end we melt exhausted into each other comfortably, like sliding mudpies or ice-cream. He shows me just enough of himself to intrigue me.

11

'Coming swimming?'

Anita swims to lose energy.

'I have so much energy I feel I might burst,' she says.

I swim to acquire energy and right now energy is what I need. He has worn me out. Swimming seems a good idea.

I stuff an old wicker basket with a towel and shampoo and warm-yellow-lensed goggles and set off on a slow meander down the road to the turquoise pool which stands in the middle of a green park.

At this time of day, three in the afternoon, the water is fairly empty. The school classes have gone home and the office workers are still buried in their termite nests. There is only one swimmer in the water: a pugnacious male crawler who ploughs through the water like a red sports car, as if his virility depended on speed.

Anita is already there, skin white as a peeled potato, unusually sunning herself on the concrete terrace which surrounds the pool. We go into the changing room and peel off our clothes.

'Ruby?' she says. Her tone is tentative. She is treading carefully and it makes me nervous.

I'm squatting down, cursing and swearing at a knotted, recalcitrant shoelace.

'Yes,' I reply.

'There's something I want to tell you.'

A few nights earlier, in the rain, outside the cinema, I hadn't guessed what she was going to say. Now, in the daylight, I have guessed her disclosure before she has spoken.

'Where?' I ask, cutting out the painful preamble. Husband and best friend: how could she?

'Here. Eight months ago . . . It meant nothing to either of us, Rue. Nothing.'

'So why do it?' I think but I don't say. Instead I go into slow motion; no words come. Robotically, I free my foot from the shoe, and I tug on my black swimsuit. Anita sits on the patchily damp wooden-slatted bench, waiting for an overt response – tears, recrimination or blind anger.

When I do speak, although I'm boiling inside, I speak flatly, revealing nothing. 'Come on then,' I say.

I need to get into the water. I am ready for another purification process, another attempt to wash the dirt away.

'Aren't you going to say anything?' she asks. It is as if she desperately needs a response, as if she might even be asking for the impossible – instant forgiveness. I don't want to react now. I want to keep my feelings to myself. 'Not yet. No,' I reply.

After the swim, which goes by in silence, and after I've achieved my twenty-length goal, I get out alone and go back into the muddy-floored changing rooms, where the walls are coloured a municipal yellow.

'I want to go to the police,' she says, rubbing her body so ferociously with a towel that the skin turns an angry rash-red. She is dishing out to her body some of the abuse she usually inflicts on others.

'I don't. Absolutely not.'

I get dressed and go to the stainless-steel mirror.

'Ruby?' she says, as I'm painting a black rim round my eyes.

'Yup.'

She comes over to me and rests her chin on my shoulders, looking at my face in the mirror.

'Sorry. I'm really sorry,' she says.

I don't want to be sucked into a discussion. Right now I couldn't do myself justice. I wriggle, pick up my basket and move away. I march home, along the pavements, on autopilot.

'Why not give it up?' he asks the next afternoon, when the phone goes and it's oily Barry wheedling me to take a lousily paid job out at Randwick, by the airport. His legs hug my waist. On the phone I drive a hard bargain, say I'll only go if my costly fares – to and fro – are paid in cash. They will be, Baz says.

'I'll pay you,' he goes, tongue in my ear. I ignore him and scribble down the client's room number and name on a scrap of paper and hang up the receiver. The job has come in and I want it.

'You hate it, don't you? Say it. Just how much you hate it.'

Emotions don't come into it. Working is a habit, a regime I've always stuck to. I don't know what I'd do without it, though I want to be without it. I try to explain all of this and it comes out garbled, without links between one point and the next.

'I'll set you up,' he says. 'You need only work for me.'

'Set up.' The words sound like 'locked up', only this lock-up would be an exclusive, satin-cushioned captivity. It's an offer to mull over, though my instant reaction is to turn it down straight away. I temper myself.

'I'll think,' I say. 'Thank you,' I add.

He checks his watch, swings his legs off the bed and pulls on his trousers. By his silence, I can tell he's annoyed, or hurt, or both. Although his time is up I feel bad, as if I'm throwing him out. I have a moment of panic: I can't afford to think like this, it is part of the old guilt seeping in, the feelings that were always there with John but which, with a client, should be strictly absent.

He lets himself out and in next to no time I am taxi-ing along straight, diesel-perfumed roads to an airport hotel.

The guy is in bed when I get to his room. He's from Tokyo and is in Sydney for two days. He arrived early morning, has been in business meetings all day and after a particularly arduous late-afternoon one decided that he deserved a woman. That's exactly the way he puts it; as if I am a prize, a reward that he has won through sheer hard work. He speaks good, though odd, English.

He heard of me on the grapevine. I saw a friend of his. When he was last in town he tried to get hold of me but I wasn't on the rota. He had seen someone else instead, Michelle, but she hadn't been right. She had been too thin, with too squeaky a voice and she hadn't smiled enough.

'Talk dirty!' he commands.

I churn out some bullshit which seems to please him.

He wants to do it twice. The second time we do it, an hour later, it hurts. I lie underneath, switch off, shut my eyes tight whilst he grinds away on top. My hands go through the motions. My spine curves. I purr. I smile and he is happy and gives me a 20 per cent tip.

When I leave, I'm in tears. I cry discreetly, dabbing my eyes so that it looks as if I am having a contact lens problem. As jobs go it was simple, so I can't quite work out exactly why I'm crying. He was clean and civil and in the hour's gap between sessions he slept like a baby and didn't demand small talk.

I want to erase each client from my memory as soon as I've left him but often he will stay, like the smell of old perfume in a coat sleeve. I fool myself that I forget, that no one encounter means anything. I put on my make-up. I stick on my smile. I pretend. I fuck. I fake it. I go home. I take off my mask. I tell myself to look in the mirror. 'This is me. Here now. In my home.'

I switch on TV. I open a newspaper. They are everywhere. They invade every space. 'They': third person plural. I generalize about them, lump them together like interchangeable brands of margarine at a supermarket.

Sometimes they don't go. There are nights when I close my eyes tight like uncooked mussels and the faces, hundreds of them, crowd in.

I delay thinking about John and Anita – what they did together and where, how often, how good it was – for as long as I can. I fool myself that if I stave off the feelings of betrayal and deceit by putting them on hold, they will eventually dissolve of their own accord, painlessly.

However, the procrastination theory doesn't work. The feelings worm through my skin layers and, when they reach my bloodstream, I find that I can't fend off the huge waves of rage and anger.

One afternoon, out in Point Piper, last winter, Anita and I had just done a job together and we had got a taxi home and we were resting, lying on the bed, half asleep, drowsing off to some music. John had come home from work early. I had camped it up, included John in a scene that he didn't really understand. Sometimes I would do that; do anything for a rise. I'd push and prod and wheedle. 'Want to join us?' I had asked, getting off the big soft bed, pulling a big white towel around me, going over to kiss him. 'You'd have to pay a lot for this but we'll give it you for free!' Part of me was still in the role that I had been playing for the last job. I hadn't switched off.

Anita had stayed on the bed, flicking through the pages of a glossy magazine. 'Hi,' she went, nonchalantly, hardly looking up. She had worked the night before and she was exhausted.

It was the first time that he had hit me. *Wham!* Right across my face. I didn't say anything. I just took it. *Wham!* Anita's presence stopped him from going too far. He shocked himself and stopped.

'Fuck . . . What was that about?' Anita had said as his car roared off down the gravel drive, throwing up the pebbles. 'Is he upset or what?'

He was upset. He was always jealous of my friendship with her. He never really understood it, always felt threatened by it, never understood that the work we did limbered us up, and that, to an outsider, it might make it look as if something else was going on.

He came home three hours later. Anita had just left and I was in the bath, surrounded by candles, trying to relax in the half-light. He came into the bathroom and pulled a chair up to the side of the bath. 'I'm sorry,' he had said.

We tried talking things through.

'I don't trust her,' he had said. 'I don't trust you and her.'

'I love her. She's my friend.'

'Do you fuck her?'

'No.'

'She would with you, wouldn't she?'

Knowing Anita, she probably would.

John just couldn't understand. 'I don't have friends like that.' He kept repeating it. 'I don't have friends like that.'

Replaying the last six months obsessively, with my diary out, hour by hour, this incident must have been bang in the middle of their affair. At the time, I had felt the one to blame. I felt as if I had done something wrong and had somehow betrayed John. Now, weaving this new information into my understanding of the way things were and how they collapsed between John and me, I feel betrayed. Both of them knew something that I didn't. They were enjoying a secret from which I was excluded.

Somehow I feel more betrayed by Anita than by John. Anita was a party to the way things were with John; I had confided in her about our troubles; she was my confidante. At the same time as she was this to me she was sleeping with him. Her behaviour has shocked me. John is past the point at which he can do that.

The fact that she is a hooker makes no difference. The fact that she, like me, opens her skinny legs like new scissors, easily and smoothly, is a thing apart. Out of work the rules that ordinary people live by and love by apply. We are no different from anyone else. 'It meant nothing!' she said, but I don't believe it. John wasn't an anonymous client. Their union, however brief, wasn't an isolated hour spent in an anonymous location between strangers. Their lives were already interlinked and, although I wasn't there, I was involved in their meeting.

12

A week goes by. John has turned silent as a gravestone. This is a quiet time; full and heavy, it is a time for brooding.

Anita phones. She's probably suffering too: I doubt that she's skimming along guilt-free. I feel that she wants to smooth things over. Each time she calls I sit still in my armchair, watch the answering machine flash and clunk into action, and listen to her disembodied voice drift out over the furniture.

Finally, when I feel I'm ready, I phone her. If we meet out of doors the sea and the wind might give something back of what she might try to take away. 'Why haven't you returned my calls?' she asks angrily. I've been underground, like a bulb beneath the earth's surface, waiting until the time feels right to come up into the light. I suggest that we meet and go to Manly for the day. She agrees in principle but holds the power for a moment and messes around with days until she comes up with a free one where she can slot me in: Saturday next, nine days' time.

Just as I'm hanging up, a string of questions springs up unexpectedly, like mushrooms overnight. 'How often?', 'Did he pay you?', 'When?', 'Where?', 'Why?' She answers me directly, in as few words as possible. I have guessed the answers before she says them.

'No news of him?' I ask, rounding the inquest off.

'None.'

'Did you get the locks changed?'

'Sure did. What d'you think I am? Stupid?'

'No calls to the radio station?'

'No. He's only gone quiet coz he's waiting, Rue. Waiting to pounce. You know that, do you?'

*

Rewind. Replay. Rewind. Replay. I watch the past frame by frame; scrutinize, judge and extract meaning from. I try to understand, to wash clean and to dispose of.

Another time, we were walking through the Botanical Gardens. It had been my idea. We were surrounded by greenery. I always want to get back to the Garden, to find the green grass in amongst the concrete dust.

John was bored from the start. He is always happier indoors. He understands bricks and mortar. Thick grey clouds began to cancel out what little light there was and it started to rain. Very quickly it was pouring. John cursed and swore and blamed me for matting up his new suede shoes. He's a vain man; he can't bear looking dishevelled.

We took cover as best as we could under the swaying fronds of a banana tree. There was nothing to do but laugh. John could never laugh when the joke, or part of it, was levelled at him: his ego is too fragile to allow a joke at its expense. Other people were running and ducking for cover, hurrying across the grass until they became small black dots, the size of currants, on the road the other side. John grabbed me by my shoulders. He began to shake me, harder and harder as if I were a rag doll. At first I thought that he was messing around – joking, mock fighting. Then I could see he couldn't stop. There was frenzy in his eyes. He shook and shook. I began to feel sick with the vibration.

'*Stop!*' I yelled. There was no reaction. 'John, *stop!*'

Finally he did stop. I fell sharply on the tree trunk, bruised my spine, grazed my knee. He stomped off over the green grass towards the shiny wet tarmac of the main road. I went home alone, by bus.

When he reappeared, five hours later, I was on my way out to a job. He had been into the restaurant and must have been drinking with the staff left over from the lunch shift. His breath smelt of Scotch. Not a word was said.

Later, when I got home from the job, we still didn't speak. By then my hot anger had cooled. I couldn't be bothered to extract

an apology and he didn't offer one. Our relationship had conge-
aled and had caked into a solid jelly, like cold porridge.

The job went well. I worked out all my wrath and frustrations
on my client, who mistook my anger for genuine passion. I went
home and slept like a baby. I offloaded my own rubbish on to a
job and did exactly what the client was probably doing to me,
only in reverse.

Two days later my gentleman comes round. All morning I've
been singing. It's been three days since we last met. I'm glad to
see him.

He asks me why I am here, displaced, on the bottom of the
world. I answer loosely; the details aren't interesting.

I came because John is a restaurateur. I came because this is
the lucky country, with fat, rounded zucchini and tight, shiny
eggplants and big, fat juicy prawns and meat in excess.

I came because of me: I was sick of working illegally, under-
cover and shamefully. I wanted to hold my head up high. I was
sick of meeting clients in windy car-parks of posh hotels in order
that snooty little jumped-up porters didn't guess what I was. I
thought it might be different here.

The sun is shining hot and yellow. The skies are blue and some
days the quality of light has a violent clarity to it.

'Will those reasons do?'

Whilst I was talking I noticed that his eyes were gliding over my
body and that he had a glazed expression on his face. Although he
asked a question, I don't feel that he listened to the answer.
Suddenly it matters that he approves. I repeat myself. 'Will those
reasons do?' He pulls me towards him, takes hold of my arms
and yanks me across the bed. He looks at me quizzically, then
responds as if he's genuinely surprised to find I need the assur-
ance I do. 'Any reasons will do,' he says.

I pull away. I want to deny him sex, though of course I can't
do this; it's what he's here for and he is paying. Sometimes I want
to lock myself away and become a nun. Instead, I give in, open
my legs, and try to seem welcoming.

Afterwards he asks, 'What's your husband like?'

I pause. I'm not sure he needs to know and I'm not sure I want to answer. I do answer but I do so from a distance, as if John is very far away, a speck of dust floating round the sun. If I do this, I find I can speak clearly and that somehow the hurt is lessened.

'John fulfilled his ambition and he doesn't know what to target next. Because he knows the way from A to B and because he could drive it blindfold, he drinks. The more he drinks, the more he removes himself from his surroundings. He has reached the point when he is living inside himself completely, an island, not a tropical one but one which comes with snow and ice, a chip off a glacier.'

My lover frowns. He looks at me down his long, graceful, aquiline nose. He has a face to be sculpted rather than painted, a face whose beauty lies in its hollows and its shadows, its bones and its curves.

'Why do you speak in poetry?' he asks.

'It comes out like that,' I reply.

'Why don't you leave? If it's that bad, why not just go? Save me the misery, John.'

This was four months ago. We were driving down the south coast for a weekend away at one of John's employees' beach houses, seven hours or so out of Sydney. We had left home at three in the morning so as to get an open road and dawn was coming up. The sea was on our left and a huge thigh of land, covered with dark-green scrub, was on our right. We passed just one vehicle in two hours. The only things on the road, every now and again, were kangaroos drawn to the car's headlights like moths.

He turned to me, took his eyes right off the road and looked me straight in the face. 'Huh?' I had gone, challenging him one step more. The car began to veer towards the left. I grabbed hold of the wheel and started to do the driving which he had opted out of.

'Because . . . Because you understand. Because you are the

only woman in the whole fucking world who understands me. OK?'

That was the truth. That was why he stayed. I stayed, I've already said, because I knew what the deal was and I was scared to jump and I'm lazy as sin.

When I'm down, I shop. I glide along the supermarket walkways like a visiting spirit. I reach nirvana – the chocolate counter. I fill a basket with all shades of the angel food: dark, white, milk. I think of chocolate melting, warm and slimy in my mouth.

At the check-out desk, stacked beside the bent wire baskets, is a pile of newspapers. 'CALL GIRL FOUND DEAD.' I freeze, read the first paragraph, freeze, read it a second time. It only half goes in. I read it a third time, take a breather, see stars, then try again. 'Yeah, luv?' the till girl says. 'Wakey-wakey.'

The photograph looks years out of date. Her thick black Afro hair is cropped short to the head whereas a month ago it hung in ringlets down to her shoulders. Charlotte's smile is the same though: a row of white pearl teeth gleam out of a dark-brown face.

She was found by a chambermaid early this morning in a luxury suite at the Intercontinental. She had been raped, tied to the bed and shot in the head and each breast three times.

13

Barry calls up an hour or so after I've got myself home. He sounds grave, pompous and fatherly. He wants 'us all' to get together this evening.

Bucks are all that count; he doesn't want anyone throwing in the towel. He doesn't want to lose his workforce overnight. He can't risk, with his fragile balancing of mortgages, remortgages, deals here and deals there, to lose a cent. Money makes his world go round.

During the evening, he misses the mark wide, on every point. First, with massive insensitivity, he had clearly wanted the gathering to be an easy-going cocktail party. Dom Perignon and canapés are wheeled in on a silver tray and Baz is dressed up rather than down in a natty little navy blazer and white trousers. None of us is purposefully kitted out in black but most of us have come as we are – tatty old jeans, scrumpled-up shirts.

Barry fast gauges our overall mood of fear, sadness and grief, and instantly becomes as solemn as we are, tactically converting his attempted chitchat into a functional speech. He coughs, stands in the middle of the room, and cuts a lone male figure in a room full of thirty or so women. Business is to carry on as usual. There is no cause for concern. Charlotte had her fingers in many pies and the murder is, most likely, domestic.

'Like fuck!' Katya, a Polish girl, mutters. 'Why the hell would anyone who knew her want to kill her in a hotel room? . . . Besides which, she was a dyke.'

Barry's retort is foolish: 'Don't women kill?' It's a quip which loses him yet more Brownie points with an already hostile audience.

'Not often!' someone else chips in.

Hotly defensive, now desperate to prove us all wrong, Barry quotes the name of a recent female serial killer from Atlanta. It's another bad move. By now we are hissing.

Barry shouts out that his deal is this: anyone who works until the end of the week will be offered a third extra pay. 'So who's going to show tough and keep on working?' Someone objects to the 'show tough' blackmail.

Bribed by increased pay, half of us decide to keep working; the other half will take time off. I go with the latter. For the next few days, until things settle, nothing would induce me to go out to work.

Next Barry brings up safety. From now on we all have to phone in, not just at the start of a session, but also at the end. He spins a yarn about how 'safe' we escort girls are, how well covered: the cops are taking Charlotte's death 'very seriously'. 'They're right behind you lot. Watching out for you. Working hard behind the scenes.'

'So why aren't they here right now? Why aren't they interviewing us?' Katya asks.

Another woman picks up on the phoning in at the start of a session plan. 'It only takes two seconds to kill,' she goes. 'We get to a job. It looks cool. We phone you and tell you it's all OK, but then the geezer gets rough and it'll take two hours, till we don't phone back when we're next meant to, for you to realize that anything's wrong. By then we're meat.'

I switch off. My mind wanders like a snooping sniffer dog. Recently two women were run over by a carload of Westies who drove drunk into town on a Friday night. Pumped up on anti-hooker venom, they aimed a car right at the girls. The women were killed instantly. The car soared off into the dark; the men got off scot-free. Amongst the community, everyone knows that the police hardly lifted a finger to catch those guys. Each weekend busloads of young studs out on stag nights drive through the Cross, dangling their bodies out of mini-bus windows, screaming abuse at any street worker they see. Often they go into parlours, come down heavy and violent with the girls, try and get sessions for free, pull knives, rob, do the works. The cops continue to do nothing. The bottom line is that the cops think we're not worth protecting. We have stepped outside society so we don't deserve the law to protect us. When something like Charlotte's death happens we all realize just how isolated and vulnerable we are. We stick together and form protection networks.

The best we can do for now is all of us refuse to see any new clients. Barry isn't happy with the idea; it means that he will lose 30 per cent of his trade, but, in the face of our opposition, there is nothing he can do. He stuffs a canapé in his face, pours another Scotch, and tells us it's time to go.

On the way home, I stop off at Anita's. I'll put aside betrayal; events are taking over. Combined with Charlotte's death, John's threats have amplified in my mind. Anita doesn't read papers. I'm worried for her. I phoned earlier, before I left home, and left a message saying, 'Call me.' She hasn't replied.

Her apartment light is on. The electronic buzzer is broken so I climb up the stairs and knock. On the other side of the door I can hear both her voice and the voice of a man speaking softly. She doesn't reply. I knock again. The voices go silent. I call out her name. She would recognize my voice. Usually, however busy she is, she would come to the door.

I remember Charlotte's voice on the end of the phone. I remember doing a job with her at a flat in Pott's Point, overlooking the harbour. The guys were dealers and there was a bin bag of grass heads in the middle of the room. We got giggly and, prancing round a ping-pong table naked, had both laughed so much that our sides had ached. It was one of those rare jobs that had gelled. I had had fun. The guys were nice, good sorts, and the job had been extended, one hour at a time, so it ended up that we did a lucrative overnight.

We left the flat at six in the morning and went up to the Cross for breakfast. She wolfed down a double focaccia, a great brick of a sandwich. She ate ravenously, as if she hadn't eaten for a week.

14

Later, I'm hypnotically stirring tomato soup with a small flat wooden spoon, round and round and round and round in the bubbling cauldron, when the phone rings. I'm in a dreamworld, not a pleasant one, a nightmare one; I'm thinking of Charlotte, the tag around her toe and the shiny steel of the mort slab. I'm feeling infected by the heavy mood at Barry's just an hour earlier. When the phone goes, I'm expecting Anita's voice with an explanation of what was going on behind closed doors.

'Cunt . . . Watch it.'

There then follows a series of groans, pauses, sighs and lastly a horrible high-pitched falsetto laugh.

'Cut it out, John.'

'Who say's it's John?'

'Come on . . . Just quit it. Forget it . . . Leave me alone.'

'Heard about Charlotte?'

A long silence opens up and sucks me down into it. I link John to Charlotte. I try to sever this connection, tell myself that my imagination is running away with me, that there's no connection at all.

'Eh? . . . Heard about Charlotte, I said. Maybe you're not hearing me. Getting the gist? C-C-C-Come to get you.'

I slam down the handset. The smell of burning additives and E numbers wafts through from the kitchen.

There are no guns at my head, no coffins on my doorstep, no knives at my throat, but I feel danger chomping at the bit, waiting to bite. Scared to the bone, imagining the knocks and creaks of floorboards to be the creaks of intruders, friends of John, friends of friends of John, I act on impulse. Despite everything I think about the cops, they are the only protection on offer. I pick up the phone and dial triple zero.

The cop who comes is a nice enough boy but boy he is – maybe twenty-three at the most. He is not big enough, tall enough, broad enough or old enough to make me feel confident. He arrives within ten minutes of the call-out and once inside the house he dangles awkwardly in the centre of the room like a broken mobile. He kicks his knees out nervously like a pony, part gesture to straighten out the creases in his trouser legs, part nerves.

I show him John's note. I tell him about the calls.

'Profession?'

'Escort.'

'Ah . . . In that case,' and he gets on to his crackly walkie-talkie, presumably because I come into a category which he can't deal with, or that other cops – older, wiser and on fatter pay cheques – specialize in.

Five minutes later, cop number two poles up. As I open the door his eyes drink in the shape of my body, drink in the curves and contours, and undress me. As if he senses my discomfort, he immediately compensates by turning on an intangible, though considerable, charm. He shakes my hand firmly. 'Al Dunne . . .' He speaks in a gravelly, Aussie accent, a voice smelling of scrub and sweat. I feel the rim of a gold ring link momentarily into my own. He looks me straight in the eye, too boldly, a little defiantly.

'Pleased to meet you,' he says. He turns to his junior. 'OK, Joe . . . I'll take care of this.'

Joe clumsily takes his leave.

'May I?' Dunne asks, pointing to a chair pulled up by the table.

I nod. He sits down and takes out a new, blue Bic biro and notepad from his jacket pocket. I draw up a hard-backed chair and sit opposite him, ready for business, face to face. He begins to spit his questions out like gunfire.

'Who do you work for?'

'Elite.'

'Know Charlotte Lemonte?'

'Yes.'

'Know Sister Scourge?'

I hesitate. He raises his eyes, quickly reacting to my delay. He gives a big, soft smile and he lowers his tone. 'I'm sorry . . . Do you? Just a yes or a no?'

Caught off guard, I reply, 'Yes.'

He nods knowingly, then changes tack.

'You've been getting these phone calls? Who do you think is behind them?'

'My husband.'

'Name?'

'John Goldman.'

I've hit a nerve; he jumps.

'Do you know of John?' I ask.

'Yup.'

'How come?'

He won't answer. He needs to know the answers to some more questions, such as where John is living, when exactly we parted company and why.

I ask, 'What business is it of yours?'

He grins like a big kid. 'None.'

He begins on the next round of questions; these ones concern Anita.

'What is your exact connection with her?'

'Friend.'

'You're thinking, "Why does he need to know about her?", aren't you? You're thinking, "Why the hell have I called out the cops about phone calls and they ask me about Sister Scourge?", aren't you?'

I nod. 'Yup. Sure am. You put the words into my mouth.'

'I need to see her too.'

He sucks the end of his pen and partially repeats himself, 'Shit, I do.' Some biro ink spills out and leaves a sticky blue blob on the crease of his lip.

Everything about this man is phoney. He seems to be composed of bit parts, none of which fuses together and makes a whole. As soon as I go firm on this assessment of him, I relax a little.

'Is there a problem with John?' I ask.

'Not that we know of,' he replies.

'Is there a problem with Anita?'

'Maybe . . . Nothing that I can expand on.'

For the time being, my phone line will be monitored. For the time being, my flat will be watched.

The fact that he takes the threats and calls seriously makes me even more scared than I already am. I notice that as soon as I disclose any fear, or show a hint of anxiety, Dunne picks up on it and digs in deeper. He rounds up the meeting with a strange monologue that sounds as if it is lifted straight from a poor cops movie and which he stands up to recite.

'There's danger out there . . . D-A-N-G-E-R. The Lemonte woman is just the beginning. I don't want you or your friend to become another statistic. Right?'

I try to be nonchalant at Dunne's plain oddness. I try to stay cool. 'Sure,' I say.

'There's danger out there,' he repeats, nodding to the closed shutters. 'You from London, right?'

I nod.

'Rats. Alleyways. Knives. Stained concrete tower blocks, harsh orange spotlights, graffitied walls, skinny sick trees, bird shit. I went to London once. Horrible. A pisshole. One big urinal.'

Until recently Sydney had felt safe. I saw it as a straightforward place, full of direct, easy, uncomplicated citizens. It was a city of primary colours where politicians even cry on chat shows. It was a sensuous city, a place to relax into, to be at ease in. I had been aware of the violence, of course I had, but in a second-hand way. Now the violence, the blackness, feels as if it has a foot inside my door.

Dunne pops his biro away in his top pocket. He walks towards the door and he pauses to check out my record collection.

'Don't like Country and Western, then?'

'No.'

He pulls his lips downwards in an upside-down smile.

'Sad. A little Pom like you who doesn't like to have her heart-strings pulled. Is that right?'

I don't reply.

He lifts his right hand up politely to his head and salutes officiously, like a US marine.

'So long.'

He is as unusual as cucumber served as a warm vegetable at the Hilton would be.

At dawn, sleepless, I nudge open the shutters. A baby-boy-blue Holden estate drives slowly past, then pulls up opposite. Its driver, a solitary gentleman, switches off the engine, brings a polystyrene cup of coffee up to his lips and turns his head to face my house. He winds down his window and stares hard.

Simultaneously my phone rings. My heart bumps. This is too early for a personal call.

'G'day. Al Dunne here.'

His voice sounds gratingly chirpy, like the voice of a main-stream radio DJ. In the background some blue grass banjo music is jangling. He must be calling from home.

The pale-blue Holden is nothing to worry about. Its driver is one of his men, 'OK, duck? OK, Miss Cox?'

'OK.'

'T'ra then.' He pauses. 'Oh, Cox as in apple. As in Pom. Geddit? T'ra.'

The line buzzes. He vanishes and I'm left with my empty, silent flat.

Two hours later my man comes round on an early pre-business appointment, an encounter to get him revved up for the busy day ahead. We are weaving and winding in bed when the phone rings again.

'Hi.'

It's Dunne.

'Your husband.'

'Yes.'

'We've run a search and nothing doing.'

There wouldn't be 'anything doing' – John hasn't got a criminal record. The most they would get about him is a couple of parking fines and maybe at best a few late tax payments. I'm confused; I explained all of this to Dunne the night before. Into the middle of my confusion, he springs another question, from an odd angle. 'Can I speak to the man with you now?' he asks.

I falter before getting clear about my standpoint. 'No . . . No you can't.'

'Fine.'

'Is there a problem?' I ask. 'About the gentleman? About anything?'

'No . . . Just an idea . . .'

And then again he suddenly hangs up.

I flop back into the pillows.

'Who was it?'

'The cops.'

He rolls over. His eyes register concern.

'You in trouble?'

'No.'

He slides his hand down and strokes my breast gently. 'Sure?'

Before I answer I need to know who he is. Before I can trust I need to know his name. I'd like to feel, for sure, that he isn't caught up in this.

'Are you an MP?' I ask.

He laughs and laughs and laughs.

'No.'

Yet he comes and goes in a Daimler. Maybe he's from Perth, maybe he owns racehorses or a fleet of aeroplanes. Maybe he owns a brewery, or a newspaper. Maybe he makes Akubra hats. Maybe he runs safaris into the national parks.

'Why won't you tell me who you are?' I ask. My voice sounds childish; it has a plaintive squeal to it.

'Does it matter?'

'I need to know before I can trust,' I reply.

'One day you'll discover it,' he says. 'One day you'll know . . .

'So why the secret?'

He looks at me thoughtfully and ruffles my hair affectionately.

'Because I don't want you to know. Because it might alter things . . . that's why.'

He says all of this sincerely. Despite his integrity and the sense that his mind is made up and he will speak no further, I needle. I still want an answer.

'Is it sinister . . . what you do?'

He is patient with me. 'No,' he replies. 'No, it's not sinister.'

A few days later he comes round again. I have spent most of the week alone, with my own mad thoughts for company. I'm lonely and scared. 'You,' I want to say, his arms curling around my shoulders, one leg flopped over my hip, cradling me asleep. 'Rescue me . . . Take me away.' Of course, I don't say the words. Given the nascent stage of our relationship, they seem too laden, too full, too romantic and too darn stupid. Also there's another reason why I keep silent; the words would be inappropriate given our business relationship.

None the less, I dream the words and in a way they come true. In a way he does rescue me. For the next four days I lose myself in a world which, with his payments, he creates.

I forget that a pale-blue Holden is pulled up outside my house, its driver scanning my front door with binoculars and beady, hawk eyes. Somehow I even forget about Charlotte. As for John, I manage to put him on hold. Thoughts of Anita's betrayal still needle me but somehow the pain is dulling. I'm near the stage when I'll be able to reach beyond it, to welcome her in again, and, I suppose, to forgive.

I begin to receive my extravagant payments. I almost slipped up there, I called them 'presents'. These aren't gifts, though. I have worked for them, slaved for them, and have even begun to open up my heart, like an eyelid gingerly opening underwater.

The first arrives early morning. I answer the door to find an Interflora man standing in front of me. May he bring the delivery in? 'Sure,' I say, thinking why the hell can't he simply hand me what he is already holding, which is an armful of roses.

But it takes him over an hour to deliver the flowers. There are

3,000 roses in all. When he leaves, every jug and container that I possess is full of them, as is the white bath, sink and wash-basin. The rest are strewn extravagantly over the floor, along the window-ledges, on every surface. The air is scented. My home smells of roses.

The second payment, delivered later the same day, that after-noon, is a box of Beethoven's symphonies, along with a brand-new CD player. It is delivered by a thin, young gentleman who delivers them under ominous 'instruction' (so he says) to install the system. This complicated wiring process takes over an hour to complete.

It is soon sequelled by the arrival of the man himself. He arrives, as is usual, in the back seat of the Daimler, but this time, unusually, he arrives with his arms full, weighed down by a flat-screened Japanese TV set.

'Watch enough and you'll see who I am,' he says, thudding the heavy machine down in the middle of the room.

Later, after he has gone, I put the television on a chair and tug it to the end of the bed. I lie back in the puffed-up pillows. I channel-switch and munch away at a juicy, warm falafel roll at the same time.

He phones.

'How's the TV?'

'Fine . . . A drug like they all are.'

Its screen is throwing out a hum and a fuzzy green light. I had fallen asleep in front of its radioactive rays.

'I want to renegotiate for more time. I will pay accordingly.'

He speaks stiffly. I have noticed that he tends to lapse in and out of extreme formality. One day he plays the first-time client, all puckered up and proper, nervous, almost embarrassed at any hint of intimacy; the next time we meet he is a lover, solicitous, wanting to discover who I am. The dichotomy that I feel with him, between being a prostitute and a lover, he feels too. His opposing roles are client and lover. Both roles co-exist uneasily with each other.

94

I agree to his request right away. 'OK,' I go, slipping into hooker talk. 'Deal done.'

The next time we meet he accidentally lets his name slip out whilst he is relating a story. The story is something about his wife, who is spoken of in the past tense. Not past as in moved onwards and upwards to better things and to heaven, but past as in past-tense divorced. The story concerns boring administrative details such as alimony. His name is Luke.

The story also contains mention of his children. There are three of them, a chorus line of girls, and they all have maid's names: Alice, Rose and Charlotte. His wife's name is something catchy and pretty ending in 'eee' – Nicky, Libbie, Katie, Susie, Jenny or Penny.

Oh, and they live in Melbourne.

Part of me wants to hear all of this and part doesn't. Information shared is information requested. His revelation will mean that I have to share more of my history and, right now, exposure seems a terrifying prospect. He does some gentle prodding and asks if I'm still married.

'Yes and no,' I reply.

Yesterday I took off the ring and flushed it down the toilet. It sank and stayed at the bottom of the toilet bowl and I had to give it ten flushes, at intervals, before it decided to shift. Right now it is probably being disgorged into the sea out at Bondi. I imagine it lodging as a gallstone in the gut of a white shark.

He tells me that I'm a good listener. This is true: I am. The profession teaches you to listen. Nod, listen, soak it all in, listen and learn.

Sometimes my body works like clockwork. He understands it exactly. He applies the exact mixture of vibration and pressure at the right time. Being with him is like being wired up to an electric current. I ripple with a series of electric shocks. His cock is perfect. It's easy to talk dirt with a client, to lie for all it's worth, which is, most likely, a big fat tip. With Luke it's hard. I feel coy, like a teenager. I feel slimy like a warm oyster when I take his dick in my mouth, feel it grow. His tongue on mine, our tongues moving

95

in rhythm to his salty cock. Then his tongue in my cunt, flicking, like the fin of a fish.

15

Next day, still no call back from Anita and paranoia setting in, I go round. She answers immediately and she is in costume. Her small elfin features are transformed into a grotesque parody of female power, her complexion caked with white pancake foundation, her body cling-filmed in a tight red PVC catsuit. With a silver zipper shooting up its front, it looks like a cheap boot picked up for next to nothing in the sales on Carnaby Street.

'Come in. Come in, doll,' she says warmly, as if all is forgotten.

'Don't doll me,' I reply, half joking, half serious. I'd rather be a duck than a doll, but preferably neither, preferably just me – Ruby.

The costume suggests company and I feel sure that I can hear sounds coming from the kitchen. 'Someone here?' I ask.

She nods. 'It's Patrick . . . he's washing up.'

She explains that then he'll have to clean the toilet, polish the chain handle and scrub the kitchen floor, and that all of these houseboy duties will take at least an hour. 'Come in,' she repeats. 'Meant to phone you later today.'

Once we are inside the living room she yells at 'Patrick' to come through. A tall balding man, wearing diapers, crawls through the door on his hands and knees. However ridiculous and puny he looks (he also has a dog collar round his neck), it's important that I don't laugh at him. To do so would throw the fantasy off kilter. I remain monotone and expressionless and Anita introduces us regally.

'This is Ruby,' she says.

He offers me a paw. I toy with shaking it, but stop when, as he raises his face to look up at me, I recognize him. The creature –

dog-cum-baby-cum-man – on the floor is Detective Sergeant Al Dunne. I'm not exactly surprised to see him; these things happen. I am more surprised at the coincidence that out of all the B & D mistresses in Sydney he should happen to have chosen Anita and that he should happen to be here now. I pretend that I have never met him and he does the same, addressing me with outdated courtesy.

'Pleased to meet you. What would you request that I call you?'

'Madam's fine by me,' I reply nonchalantly.

'Haven't you finished the washing-up yet?' Anita snaps.

'No, Mistress.'

'Why not?'

'Because there's a lot to do,' he says with a simper and a thin-lipped smile.

Anita scowls back. Patrick probably hit a nerve; she is always sensitive over her lack of kitchen hygiene. Her kitchen is usually filthy, every surface covered by dirty crockery, cheesegraters flecked with hardened cheese and black charred saucepans.

'Might it not be because you're not fucking good at it, you stupid oaf? Isn't that the truth behind your tardiness?'

'Yes, Mistress. I think it is,' he replies.

'Yes and what?'

'Yes and you are always right. I am hopeless at doing the washing-up.'

'Yes. You're no good at anything,' she adds, sighing and glowering down at the flinching Patrick.

I am hoping that this tedious banter won't spin out for too long, and thinking that it could do since it is all part of what Dunne is paying for, when she orders that, before moving on to the bathroom, he fetch us two mugs of 'perfect' coffee.

'D'you know who he is?' I ask as soon as he is out of earshot.

'Nah. What does it matter?' she replies.

'Vice Squad big-wig. Who's paying who, Anita? He paying you or you him?'

She reacts angrily, objecting to my insinuation that she might be giving a freebie, and that, even if she was, she wouldn't have told me about it. According to her, Patrick is 'dumb and cool'.

At that stage Dunne reappears, managing to crawl on three paws and using the fourth to balance a cup of hot coffee. Anita sends hers back; the water isn't hot enough. Laboriously, he returns a second and a third time and finally, fourth time lucky, he gets it right.

'Heard about Charlotte?' I ask when he has finally left us, having dutifully dispatched the perfect cup of Nescafé.

She nods.

I carry on. 'I called in the cops. I got scared and I called them in.'

She raises an eyebrow. 'And?'

'And the guy in charge is your friend Patrick.'

'Oh.'

A few seconds later Dunne interrupts us again. Like a tiny child with its mother, he offers Anita the perfect distraction from our threateningly difficult conversation.

'I've finished, Mistress. I implore of you to come and check that my work is perfect.'

'It won't be. It'll be fucking hopeless. Everything you do is hopeless. Without hope.'

Reluctantly, with a dramatic sigh, she climbs out of the comfortable armchair, slips her feet into her boots, zips them up slowly, and totters through into the kitchen, kicking him very lightly in the butt so that he crawls faster. I overhear the kitchen conversation – they banter on about specks of dust stuck to lids of jamjars. I hear her grudgingly pass his work 'B– ' and send him off to the bathroom.

'And then what, Mistress?'

'And then I tie you up and beat you and you show me what a shrivelled little thing you are.'

'Oh, Mistress, I would like that very much indeed.'

'Good.'

She comes back into the room and slams the door behind her. She is injected with a shot of energy. The transaction with Dunne has involved, in some way, a mutual receiving and a mutual giving. She bounces on the balls of her feet.

'So why the po face? Ease up, Rue. The bloody world isn't going to fall apart. What's wrong?'

'Him,' I reply.

'He's cool,' she goes, nodding towards the bathroom, where a brush scrubs the tiled floor. 'We've got stuff over him. We know who he is. We're safe. We've got vital information.'

In this power game he has power over us too, or at least over Anita. Just by revealing her Sister Scourge identity he could lose her her radio job and maybe turn the darling of the airwaves into newspaper fodder.

'Still on for Saturday?' I ask, thinking of the sea and thinking of a day out away from all of this. Anything to do with John, any problems Anita and I might have had because of him, suddenly seem small as chickenfeed. Betrayal pales into insignificance beside the complexity of what we are being drawn into.

'Sure,' she replies.

Dunne must be coming to a close with his bathroom duties. I take my leave. I want to avoid having to take half-hearted part in his fantasy. I resent giving the creep any kicks for free and just my presence here in this flat will be upping his humiliation and embarrassment levels.

She catches my shoulder as I go out.

'You OK?'

'I'm functioning. You?'

'Cruising,' she replies, grinning. 'Just cruising.'

PART THREE

16

I watch TV. I use it like a drug – to hold real life at bay. I use it in a way I once used sex, or alcohol even – to forget, to fog over. I watch anything – chat shows, news programmes, cartoons and ads. One of the programmes I hit on by accident is an interview with an ex-pro, Claudia, by a chirpy, toupeed, chat-show host.

Claudia gave up working four years ago. She is in her late thirties and she is attractive in a homely kind of way. She has long, curly, mouse-brown hair and she is wearing an African print shirt and what look like voluminous culottes. I can imagine her tending a herb garden, growing basil, rosemary and sage, but I can't imagine her on a job. Even me, an insider, I am still hooked to bottle-blonde, leather and lace stereotypes.

What she is saying is how, in pagan times, men came to the whore, the wicca, the wise woman, the prostitute or priestess, to be given to, to be healed. The whore was a respected member of society and her work was seen as a profession which a young girl was trained to enter into. The whore understood herself to be a gifted member of the community – one through whom young men were initiated into manhood and one with whom older men found a measure of tranquillity. Claudia argues that today's hooker performs the same function but is never acknowledged for it. Society fears her, spurns her, rejects her, yet fundamentally needs her. Because society is so confused as to the whore's value, the hooker herself becomes confused as to her own virtue.

What she says is right. I feel the same way. I have become infected by other people's view of my profession and I sometimes feel the way they do about one of my kind – dirty. Claudia asks for more workers to come out of the closet and to be open with their friends and family about what they do, be proud of it. 'Be proud. Pride is power.'

After the programme goes off the air, I consider contacting her. She runs an ex-pro network. I decide against it. First, it would be a premature move: I still am a prostitute. Second, above all, the thought of being in a group of women terrifies me. I'm scared of them; they might be angry. They might rip me apart. If they have been hookers and know my story, this is unlikely. But what is likely is that they might want to tear men, whom I've loved and hated and lusted after and have understood all my life, apart.

Quitting is like quitting cigarettes; my way was to cut down slowly until I was hardly smoking at all. I'm weaning myself off slowly, like a baby from a mother's breast.

17

I meet Anita and Wayne down at Circular Quay, Saturday morning as planned, at the fish and chip stand. It's ten a.m. and she's eating a tray of Tasmanian scallops and swishing down the greasy orange batter with Diet Fanta. She fills her body with crap but she's always skinny, always has the body of a boy. I hug her and there's no warm flesh, just bones stuck together at odd angles, like twigs in a bird's nest.

My own body is changing form, slowly assuming a different identity. My hips are beginning to spread and my tummy is rounded, an upturned saucer. No one has commented on these changes but I notice them and, as I look at Anita in this harsh early morning light, I feel a twang of jealousy. There are no lines on her face or on her neck and her body is bulge-free and linear, composed of straight, firm lines.

We battle through a crowd of dawdling Japanese tourists and climb on to the Manly ferry. We sit outside on the windy deck, top front, sipping strong stewed tea from polystyrene cups and nibbling the fruit cake that they sell in the ship's kiosk. Anita smokes heavily. As soon as the scallops are swallowed, she shoves something else in her mouth: a cigarette, a cup of tea, a bite of cake, chewing gum.

'So, how've you been?' she asks as soon as we're settled down and the ship is pulling away from dry land.

'Tired.'

'You're always tired.'

'And you?'

'The same.'

She squints her eyes and looks straight ahead, out to sea.

'Heard from John?' she asks.

'No.'

'He's been calling the station again, Rue. I can't fucking handle it. If it goes on, I'll lose my job. Once was enough. Now people are beginning to get suspicious. Geezers coming up to me and asking who this Sister Scourge woman is. At the moment it's all nods, nudges and winks, but soon one of them will take it seriously – then the whole bloody world will know who I am.'

'Take some time off,' I suggest. 'Go underground for a while.'

'Might do.'

Then she changes tack. 'What have you been up to? What are you going to do?'

'Give it up,' I reply.

'Then?'

I shrug my shoulders.

The ferry is now in the middle of the harbour. I focus on the sea, on the gap between the heads which marks the start of the harbour and the start of the open ocean. The boat dips and ducks; this is the only part of the journey when we are exposed to the swell of the ocean.

'Grow flowers. I'll grow great fat yellow sunflowers and poppies and delphiniums and sit in my garden and watch them slowly grow and let no one else inside.'

'Romantic . . . And the knight in shining armour come to rescue you from the land of vice, where's he?'

The crossing takes about forty minutes and we finally dock beside the old wooden pier and shuffle off, go past the hand-painted signs to the aquarium, cross the road and walk through the tacky shopping mall which smells of candy floss towards the beach. Neither of us speaks. It is as if we have both been through an accident. The car has come off the road and we're in a state of shock. We haven't seen one another properly for weeks. The last time was with 'Patrick'. Before that there was all the stuff about John and her. There seems to be so much to discuss and to wade through that neither of us knows where to start.

We go past a furniture shop. Stacked outside on the pavement are some peculiarly ugly tables.

'Seen Sam?' I ask.

'Yup . . . When I need to.'

'Is that often?'

'Enough,' she snaps, angry at the subject matter.

The beach is neither crowded nor empty; there are maybe sixty people in sight. They are all doing things – walking dogs, playing frisbees, flying kites or surfing. It could be Europe – an unglamorous Channel beach or somewhere in Holland maybe, where the families struggle with stripy canvas windbreaks and where kids build castles out of muddy sand, wearing white knickers, whilst their mums and dads sit in the shade, reading the papers. That's what it is like here today – not an iota of Mediterranean ritz. The only specifically Australian thing about this urban beach is the surfies; lying on their boards about 100 metres out, waiting for a big one.

We walk along the promenade, towards the far end of the beach where the boardwalk turns into a path and where, if you follow it for long enough, you reach a small cove which is too far a walk for most people to bother with. The cove is much more sheltered than the main beach. It's plenty warm enough to sit down – especially since we are both wearing thick, lined, English leather jackets.

We must have been there about half an hour when we see him. I'm lying on my tummy, looking back towards the promenade rather than out on the ocean and I see a tall, thin, lanky man walking very purposefully along the path towards the beach. The first thing I notice is his stride: he is walking deliberately, the way a businessman walks to the bank during his lunch hour. He's not taking things easy, and on the beach anything other than a relaxed frame of mind seems to be accentuated. I nudge Anita, who is lying back in the sand and who has her eyes shut. Dunne jumps down off the wall and on to the beach and marches across the sand very fast towards us.

She sits up. 'Oh, fuck . . . Oh, fuck.'

He is in uniform, which makes the matter of how to view him, in what light and in what role, easy. He is very clearly Detective Sergeant Al Dunne today. When he comes close enough for greetings, Anita is initially cautious and stilted with him. This is the first time that she has seen him in uniform and his role change is throwing her off-centre. She doesn't know who to pitch conversation at; whether it should be to Dunne or to 'Patrick'.

'Hi . . . Is there a problem?' she asks aggressively, as Sister Scourge might.

He nods to her, then nods a 'G'day' to me.

I sit up and wrap my leather jacket around me. Once I am vertical, a fierce sea wind grazes my face. Dunne squats down beside us.

'What's up?' I ask.

There have been more threats at the radio station. Anita needs police protection.

Also, John has been tracked and in the last week has been seen buying a gun in the Cross. He has made a series of suspicious moves. First, he has rented a room at the Intercontinental and has left home to stay in the hotel. He goes out at night, just takes the car out and drives for hours on end. He cruises William Street and shouts insults at the girls.

Secondly, there was an incident with a hooker in the Intercontinental's lift last night. John had got into the lift beside her and had asked, 'You working?' She hadn't responded. 'I know you are,' he had said. She had ignored him. He had challenged her, 'Aren't you talking?' and she had quipped, 'Not to creeps like you, no.' At that point he had fallen against the mirrored wall, one arm on either side of her body, so that she couldn't move. He had brought his lips up to her eyes and had muttered his mantra, 'Fucking slut.'

The girl had stayed very still and hadn't moved. The lift had stopped and as its door slid open, on the fifth floor, John had let her go. 'Next time,' he had said as she shuffled out, 'Next time I won't let a bitch like you go free. Next time I won't let a girl like you go into the night, getting money for nothing and going

108

home to screw up some poor lover's life, like mine.' She had immediately gone down to the reception area and had called the police. For once they had taken a prostitute's report seriously enough to follow it up.

'I'm worried about youz . . . This John guy is flipping.'

'Can't you arrest?'

Anita's question seems reasonable – far too reasonable for Dunne to agree to.

'Not yet . . . He hasn't done anything yet.'

'Can't you fucking allow us the privacy of a day on the beach?' she asks.

He shakes his head.

'Not when a butcher is out and about, sharpening his knives. Not when the bogeyman is stalking the streets.' Then he lapses into subservient talk. 'I can't risk your safety, o Mistress mine. I can't bear to think that you might be hurt, that harm might befall you.'

'Shut up,' she replied. 'Just shut up.'

We get a lift back into town in his car. The car is a regular brown Corvette, so popular amongst Dunne's colleagues that it might as well have VICE SQUAD emblazoned across its bonnet. We sit in silence, interrupted by Dunne opening up the glove compartment, revealing a hefty Country and Western cassette collection. Soon the dulcet voice of Tammy singing 'D-I-V-O-R-C-E' warbles out of the four speakers.

I sit in the back seat. Wayne squats beside me, poking his nose out of the window snootily. Dunne nods to the dog in the rear mirror.

'He get carsick?'

This is a man who takes cleanliness too seriously: his car is as sterile as the inside of a show-case fridge.

'My dog never gets carsick,' Anita replies, which is bullshit; the dog hates motion and recently there was an unfortunate incident inside a taxi.

As we slide along through suburbia into town, Dunne explains the deal. It is the same as mine. There will be someone outside her flat twenty-four hours a day and someone will follow her wherever she goes.

'Oh great! Just what I bloody need,' she replied.

She needn't talk to the tracker. She can carry on as if he isn't there, but he will be there like a lighthouse and therefore she is safe.

Dunne leaves us at the door. Upstairs, in her flat, the windows are shut and the air smells musty and dank.

The answering machine is flashing out two messages. We play them through and the wispy voice of an ingratiating client comes on.

'Please, Sister Scourge, this is Slave David. Please, please, please, I beg that I may be granted time with you. A session. You know that I pay well. Please, please, please be so kind as to phone me back. You have the number. Thank you.'

'That guy's a creep,' she says.

The second client sounds altogether more confident, more imaginative and more of a character.

'Sister, this is Slave John. I would welcome a chance to lick your beautiful ankles, to rest my head on your squeaky red plastic skirt, to let you spank me with the hedgehog spikes of a Mason and Pearson hairbrush. I look forward to receiving your hot-candlewax treatment. I looked forward to patting the head of your unleashed, wild and crazy dog. I beg of you to phone me back as soon as you can. Slave John. Mercy. Grant me mercy.'

She smiles affectionately and switches off the machine. I sink into the sagging sofa. I think of Charlotte, of John, of Dunne, of the calls to the radio station, of the web closing in around us. Sometimes, for the odd half an hour, I can forget that I'm being tracked, but then suddenly the reality comes rushing back.

'Where is it gonna end? How?'

'I don't know,' she replies softly. 'We just keep carrying on as we are, I guess.'

Wayne lollops into the room and starts to rummage round my bare feet with his wet nose. I nudge him off. You're either a dog person or a cat person and I've never liked dogs; puppies remind me somehow of premature ejaculation. Wayne, with his massive drooling jaw and short stubby tail and the peculiarly maternal approach he elicits from his mistress, acutely irritates me.

'Can't you fucking feed him or something? Tell him to buzz off?'

'Sure,' she replies. 'What's your problem, Rue?'

She gets up and comes back with a tin of old horse and a bowl. Once the tin is opened a smell of gaseous, foul meat spreads through the room. Wayne is happy. He gobbles up the food, then saunters off into the kitchen to his bean-bag bed on the kitchen floor.

'Think we're safe?' I ask. I want her input. I need support. With her problems, she can't give it. Besides which, she doesn't know any more than I do.

'We are as safe as we can be,' she says. 'Nothing can make us any safer, that's for sure.'

I cab it home. Luke is back tomorrow. Thank God for him. Thank God our arrangement is working out as it is meant to, one step at a time, logically, as we both agreed. Thank God for the brick walls of the house I think as I put the key in the latch and turn it and the door opens and inside everything is as it always was. Thank God for things and persons which stand still.

We make love to the sound of Beethoven's Eroica symphony. These huge sounds are new to me.

One of his fantasies is for me to be Josephine and he to be Napoleon. The music is a forerunner of the fantasy which we enact the following day, by which time a wardrobe full of costumes has arrived, by taxi, from a costumier's which supplies the Opera House.

I put on the costume three hours early and swan around in it, getting into the regal feel, sipping lapsang souchong tea out of a white china teacup whose brim is finely painted with gilt oak leaves. The dress I choose is exquisite. It is yellow silk, with a low-cut bosom, and it is decorated with soft moss-green silk inserts. Although there's a lot of material in the dress, it feels very light, and although the bodice is tight, it feels comfortable, as if I'm wearing nothing but a silk slip. The wig, black-ringleted, isn't so pleasant to wear. I tug it on, strut around for five minutes, feel hot and sweaty and pull it off. The door bell rings and I yank it on again.

He arrives in swashbuckling costume too: a triangular hat, a navy-blue overcoat and cream jodhpurs broken at the knee by black leather riding boots with pointed, square toes.

The fantasy works visually but falters on the historical small talk. I've not swotted up on my battles lost and battles won and I can't repartee to the political innuendoes. We end up roaring with laughter and rolling about like fallen apples on top of the bed, which is low-lying, Japanese and non-Napoleonic.

'Your wish is my command, my Josephine,' he says, momentarily stepping back into the fantasy as we lie back exhausted in the cushions.

'Buy me a new bed!' I order.

The next day one arrives – tall, four-postered, brass and perfect. I install it in the bedroom and I lie on it all day long, beaming.

My emperor, my Napoleon, my Luke, my conquistador, my conqueror, sends other gifts too. The delivery of a walk-in wardrobe of a refrigerator is followed, an hour or so later, by the delivery of three crates of fine French champagne. The odd grand or two also arrives, crisp notes stuffed into cheap brown envelopes, delivered by ordinary post. Flowers come too, not only red roses but yellow mimosas, their blooms the texture of soft snowballs, and tongues of irises and some pale-pink carnations.

The fantasies are fun, but I'm coming to see them as ruses, enabling us to avoid developing any deeper relationship. They are thin masks; they won't last indefinitely.

My body as a main means of communication won't last indefinitely either. In the past, I have relied on it alone. My flesh was like glue; it held things together. With John, my skin and bones were enough. They got hot. They conducted electric shocks. They bounced them back. My body transmitted and received signals. I thought that I might get away by just using it alone, by wallowing in it, by working through any hitches that there were between us through sex. We just had, or didn't have, sex.

The old ways of interacting aren't enough. They have their limits and their borderlines seem to be looming closer. Luke and I are at them now. We are standing on either side of a muddy brown river, weighing up the pros and cons of jumping in. The water between us has a soup-like consistency, thick and viscous like prophylactic jelly. To get through it requires a supreme effort that needs all the tools and assets which we possess to be brought into play.

Hookers, Nina once said, are emotional virgins. They have a sexually based maturity, not an emotional one. They need to bring both into line with each other and then they will be whole.

We were in the park and it was one of those Thursday pay-days. We were sitting beside the Albert Memorial and it was a hot August afternoon. The grass was dry and sand-coloured. Nina knew a lot but she flaunted that wisdom. She put it all out on show and she intimidated me.

18

I have been cooped up in my home for two days, cooped up with pale-blue Holden hawk-eye watching me from the road, invading my privacy. Barry phones. He badly needs someone to do a job for a friend of his. 'Please, Ruby, please,' he drawls. 'For me . . .'

As it happens he catches me on the hop, bouncing off the walls in frustration; I want an out, and despite Dunne, Charlotte, Anita, despite this crazy world, I say 'Yes.'

As if to prove I shouldn't be doing it, the job is lousy. As if God is trying to get through to me with the message 'Ruby, quit now!' the job leaves a bad taste.

It takes place out at a flashy fortress-cum-mansion in Point Piper. Another agency girl, Susie, is with me; she has been hired to service my client's younger brother. The only plus to the whole evening is that I don't have to fuck the guy. He is too far gone on coke and booze for that.

Susie tries her best, writhing around the Dallas-esque living room in a fake Egyptian belly dance, trying every trick in the trade to make their rubbery pricks hard. Nothing works. The guys get angry and start blaming us. The younger one complains that our tits are too big. 'Why the hell didn't you ask for one with small ones?' he asks his brother, who in turn shrugs his shoulders and puts the blame on us. 'What's wrong with you girls?'

Susie isn't known for her diplomacy. She is too raw and honest for that. By this stage, what little patience she started off with is wearing thin.

'You,' she snaps. 'What's wrong with you?'

'What's that?' my dwork goes. I doubt that he is a man who can take a snub easily with a hard dick, let alone with a soft one.

He caught half of what she said and he is lumbering into action like an old lawnmower.

'What did you say?'

Susie takes two. Nerves swill around in my gut. This is a flash palace. There's probably a revolver kept loaded in every room. The drugs and drink have put the man on a knife edge; he could topple off it at any point.

Very slowly, Susie moves over to him. The only card which she has left to play is seduction and she plays it for all it's worth.

'Nothing,' she replies softly. 'I said nothing at all.' She smiles, puts her arms around his waist, puts her lips up to his ears and whispers something. The room is silent; no one dares move. Even the younger brother has lost his colour and is ashen-faced, focusing his attention on the couple and wondering whether Susie will pull it off. Then the man responds positively to something she says. He smiles as she sinks down on her knees; whatever nonsense she came up with did the trick.

Whilst the two of them are screwing on the sofa, I go into the bathroom for a breather. Now that we have swopped clients, I have to pump myself up for some action with the younger brother, who, thinking he wouldn't be my partner, I have largely ignored all evening. I close the bathroom door. After a wash and a pee I try to open it; the lock is jammed tight.

No one hears me banging and screaming. I bang and bang and bang and shout and scream until, two hours later, the younger brother wakes up and needs to use the bathroom. He opens the door, looks baffled to see me, and I am released.

The evening started off a two-hour booking and ended up a six-hour one. I get home at five thirty a.m. with two hours' pay, just a snivelling 150 bucks cash in hand for all that hassle, all that effort.

Next day, when my head is throbbing with sleep deprivation, Dunne phones. He is abrupt and functional. 'Dunne here. I'm coming over.'

There is no 'Please may I?' or 'Is it convenient?' but just an 'I'm coming over.' I am reminded of John's bull-headed way of making

115

decisions. Once he had made one, that was it; there was no room for niceties or negotiation.

Ten minutes later a siren screeches to a halt outside my front door. Dunne has arrived, playing cops and robbers in Glebe's quiet and leafy glades. I let him in and he cracks on with business as if he is reading off an autocue.

'I want you to see Goldman. We'll be here. I want to set it up.'

'Why?'

'We want to see if he'll bite the bullet. Want to hear how he is with you. You don't mind, do you? Isn't that what you girls do for a living – give favours?'

The man is an arsehole. I can't bear to look him in the face. I stare at the floor and I study his black lace-up shoes. Underneath his grey Crimplene trousers, he is wearing red and white polka-dot socks.

'I'll think about it,' I say, refusing to rise to his bait.

He takes out a cigarette, sits down and taps the fag on the wooden chair-arm. He lights up, taking an elephantine inhalation. Two puffs later he asks, 'Will you or won't you help me out?'

'I said I'll think.'

I want him to go. I don't want him in my house. I stand up, feeding him a cue. Feeding him an even bigger one, I say, 'If that's all.'

He stands and begins to pace the room rhythmically. He goes round it once in a slow circle and shows no sign of leaving.

'I said, "Is that all?" ' I repeat.

'You women,' he lashes out.

'Yes?' I say coolly, aware that if I let him carry on with his diatribe, he might go too far and if he does, and he makes a fool of himself, I'll have one up on him. Following my knowledge of 'Patrick', any relationship with Dunne will be about one-upmanship or power politics.

He continues, 'You have to hold the power, don't you? . . . You're both the bloody same. You and her. Have to call the bloody shots.'

116

The man's absurdity doesn't shock me; it is what I've come to expect. Every time I have met him he has wavered on the borderline of excess. The first time, within a single half-an-hour period, he played at being kindly cop, seducer and plain oddball. The second time I met him, he crawled across Anita's dirty carpet in diapers. At Manly, the third time, he played a hyperactive detective whose head was spinning from a new lead – the news that John had moved into the Intercontinental. There is no backbone to Dunne's character, no single trait, no smile, laugh, no gesture, that one can identify him by. He is an amalgam of ludicrous bitparts or caricatures, any of which might suddenly take centrestage. He needs to be handled carefully and impersonally.

He grits his teeth and says dogmatically, 'I need you to see him.'

Then he delivers a hefty portion of blackmail – a long, long laden pause.

'I need you to see him because the man is dangerous.'

There follows another enormous, weighty, guilt-ridden pause.

'If you see him, we can wire you up and if we wire you up, we might be able to get a better angle on him . . . Right?'

'I said I'll think.'

Luke visits. The TV is still at the end of the bed and we lie watching it. The close of a soap comes on and he channel-switches just before it is over. I'm inside the character's head at the time, engrossed in her personal pregnant, unmarried trauma and he switches at a crucial minute. I grab the controls and blip back to the station but the moment has vanished and has been replaced by a newsflash of a freak flood in the red centre. 'Shit!' I'm angry. He must have seen that I was watching. 'You don't watch soaps, do you?' he asks disdainfully, indifferent to my feelings. 'Do you?'

The next time he comes round things don't go too well. I feel myself withdrawing; to feel myself doing so is painful. I'm not even sure why I'm doing it. Whereas before it had been his silence and reticence which had caused a block, now it's mine.

'What's going on?' he asks, just after we've made love. 'Something is. I can feel your tension.'

'I can't explain,' I say. 'I want to but I can't.'

He gets up and gets dressed. He thwacks a wedge of dollar notes down on the bedside table and says quietly, under his breath, 'If you're going to play the hooker, I'll play the client.'

'Luke?' I go. He is hovering at the door, about to leave. 'Wait!'

He lifts an eyebrow wearily. 'Yes?'

I feel I want to rush in and smooth over. Instead I burble out some abstract lines.

'Big stuff's happening. I'm not talking to you about it; I'm not talking to anyone. I'm not deliberately excluding you, it's just that I need to keep what's happening to myself right now. OK?'

'See you later,' he says softly.

I sink into the pillows. My face crinkles up and I begin to cry.

A few hours later, when I have calmed down, I reconsider Dunne's request. I decide that if it is going to help them find out who killed Charlotte, I'll see John. If I'm covered, no harm can come to me.

I call up Dunne. In the background I can hear the comforting sound of normal office life – the clatter of computers printing out, phones ringing, background conversations.

'The answer's yes,' I say.

'Thank you. That makes my job easier.'

The next night I suffer another bad job. The guy wants his money back. His use of my body, of any woman's body, should come for free. When I refuse him, he shouts and screams, 'You fucking cunt! You money-grabbing cunt!'

I am pulling on my stockings, getting ready to go, when he starts his histrionics. My bag is beside the bed with the two fifty bucks which he has already given me stuffed inside it. He yanks it off the table, rifles through it, takes out the money.

Once I might have fought. Now I snatch the bag back, leave the rapist his money and run.

19

Anita goes off the air for a few days. She has been offered a lucrative embassy job and is making perverse love with a diplomat in Canberra.

Thursday morning, first thing, the phone rings. She is calling from a noisy kiosk outside Central Station. She is upset. On the train journey back into Sydney, whilst she was sleeping, she had a suitcase full of favourite, treasured, gear stolen. 'None of it would have happened if I hadn't been so tired. I've not slept for forty-eight hours. Can I come round?'

When she arrives one of her eyes is black and bruised and the good eye is bloodshot and overworked. I ask, 'What the hell?'

She explains that she had a tussle with the minder who had tracked her up to Canberra. He had vaulted an embassy wall and had subsequently lingered around the garden, setting off security alerts and causing her great embarrassment. When she told him that he wasn't needed, he had replied that he was working 'under orders', that he was obeying 'Sergeant Dunne' and that he would stay 'come what may'. Wearing her knuckleduster silver rings, Anita had socked him in the eye. Unprofessionally, he had hit her back. She tips her head towards the road. 'That's the git there.' A tree-trunk man is guarding the gate.

'*Go away!*' she yells at the top of her voice across the quiet road. '*Leave me alone!*'

The tree-trunk man ignores her and my man, the one in the pale-blue Holden with gleaming hubcaps, nods and grins.

She blinks and her lilac eyes fill up with tears. 'Come on,' I say, trying to calm her down, steering her away from the window and towards a seat. 'Come on.'

She brings her bony elbows up on to the table-top and drops her face down into the palms of her hands, and she begins to sob.

A stream of unedited words and emotions floods out. She is scared. She sees no escape. She feels lousy. She needs help. When there is nothing more to say and the saying has somehow washed her clean, she lies down and for the next four hours she sleeps like a baby.

Whilst she is asleep I pick up the phone, put it down again, pick it up a second time, flirt some more with it, and finally dial John's number. I get through to my own voice, which he still hasn't changed, on the answering machine. Then his voice barges through, over mine.

'Yeah?'

He agrees to meet easily, not in a café ('I find them claustrophobic') but at a strange venue – opposite the Opera House, Lady Macquarie's Chair, at six tonight sitting on top of the old stone wall. 'And don't bring any of your men with you, Ruby. Understand?'

I'm not sure if he means Dunne's gang or not but I skim over his request like a dragonfly over water, as if he's said nothing untoward. 'Sure,' I go.

At six I am in the park, sitting on the wall that overlooks the harbour. My legs dangle over the edge and my skirt turns green with the damp furry moss. To the right are the points and pricks of the Opera House, and behind me the various greens of the Botanical Gardens. Straight ahead the city's glass-fronted skyscrapers fringe the picture, their bold, corporate fronts glinting in the pink evening light. The sun, with about an hour to go before nightfall, glows big and orange. A few joggers quietly pad past in foamy rubbery shoes.

I am wired with a device that is taped to my breastbone. One of Dunne's men, Ian, sits on a bench about 40 metres away, looking out to sea and listening, at this stage, to my heartbeat through a pair of Walkmanesque earplugs.

John is late. Immediately, I suspect that he won't show up. He does and I'm surprised.

He kisses me and jumps on the wall beside me. He seems utterly at ease, as regular as a block of Wall's Cornish ice-cream.

'How've you been?'

I see him as he once was – friendly, warm and affable.

'Good . . . You?'

'Good too.'

Then he comes up with the most unexpected sentence. His words seem to be somehow not his own; I reel at their very ordinariness: 'I stopped the threats . . . It got boring.'

'Sure did,' I reply.

'I'm sorry, Ruby . . . I kinda flipped.'

I don't trust John's apologies, or his reason. I want to recoil, to run away. I take the papers out of my handbag and pass them to him. 'I need you to sign these.'

He takes them, see what they are, grunts, puts them on one side and puts his arm around me.

'It's beautiful down here . . . Remember when we first came here. Remember how we loved it here.'

By this time I feel distinctly uncomfortable. I try to move away off up the lichen-covered wall, but before I quite manage it, his hand has gone up my skirt and the next thing is that he has forced one of his fingers inside me, so roughly that it hurts. I yelp and jump off the wall.

He reacts utterly calmly, as if he has done nothing wrong, quite oblivious to my anger.

'Can't we try again?' he asks.

I brush the moss off the back of my skirt and ignore his question. I don't want to risk making him angry; I want to leave in one piece. I keep things straight and businesslike. I nod to the papers. 'Can you sign them and send me them?' I say, retreating.

'Hey, you!' he shouts like a brickie as I disappear off up the pathway towards the centre of town.

I turn.

'Nice arse!'

I kick off my shoes and run across the huge expanse of green grass until I reach the road.

When I get home, Anita is still there, watching TV, curled up on the sofa in front of the electric fire.

'Dunne called. He left a message. "It was superb." What's going on, Ruby? What haven't you told me about?'

I explain about the meeting. She's angry. She doesn't like the feeling that somehow I have gone behind her back.

'What the hell did you do that for? What good did it do you?'

'Nothing, but John is dangerous and whilst there's a possibility that he is behind what's happening out there, it's my duty to help the police to sort it out.'

Later that night, her daggers are drawn, her talons spiked and she is looking out for trouble. We have just downed a bottle and a half of rough red wine. The phone goes. I take it in the other room. It's Luke and she puts two and two together.

'Who are you seeing? Who's footing the bill. Someone must be.'

Until now I haven't mentioned Luke to her. I still don't want to. Something about him is precious and personal.

'Heh?'

I don't reply.

'Miss Mystery . . .' she goes sarcastically.'OK . . . OK . . . Don't fucking burn me with your eyes.'

After a few seconds she apologizes. 'Jeez, I'm sorry. I'm fucking sorry. I don't know what's fucking wrong. It's all getting to me like it's all getting to you.'

20

The next morning Luke knocks on the door, grabs my arm and informs me that we are going out to lunch.

I'm not expecting him. Just by turning up unannounced, he is stepping outside the contract; that is, if we still play by its rules, which I suppose we do until it is formally renounced.

'I need to talk,' he says. He speaks so emphatically and bluntly that I find myself scurrying into the house, grabbing my coat and obeying. 'I need to talk now!' he repeats, as he shuffles me, dazed and frightened, like a hostage, into the car.

'OK,' I reply, as if everything is swimming. In a way it is swimming: I feel as if I am moving slowly underwater with my eyes open. My vision is bleary. The driver starts up the car and we glide into the city in silence.

He chooses to eat at a darkly lit French restaurant where the clientele are businessmen talking school tie and deals. The room is cold and functional and the atmosphere is dry, as if no one is here for pleasure; they are all here because of work.

Last night on the phone he had been distant; he had murmured something about needing to talk. Looking at him over the crisp white napkins, which poke out of the wine glasses in starched triangular points like capable Ward Sisters' caps, I sense that the 'talk' he requested might boil down to the single word 'Goodbye.' If this is the case I'm half prepared for it. This past week things have been slightly askew. It's not that our wires have been crossed; rather that they need to cross. They have been running along in insulated casing, in self-contained parallel lines.

His approach is direct.

'What's going on?' he asks flatly. 'What's happening? I need the hell to know.'

He means business and I know that he won't settle for anything but the full story. He wants to know the reason for my moodiness, for Anita having picked up the phone the other day, for the strange nocturnal phone calls, for the eyes of the driver of the pale-blue hovering Holden. I feel that I have been kidnapped. I won't be released until I speak the truth.

If this thing between us is to carry on, I'll have to open my mouth. I decide to speak now.

I start at the beginning. I tell him how I left John; the bruises. I explain who Anita is; the chains. I explain Dunne's kinky, dual identity and I explain how he links into the story. I don't edit. I tell the whole truth as I see it. I tell it straight and honestly.

Whilst I'm speaking Luke sits still. He doesn't interrupt and he shows no signs of visible reaction, be it shock, or horror, or surprise, at what I'm saying. When I finally come to a close he speaks softly, with concern. 'I didn't realize. Why didn't you say?'

Immediately I feel guilt that I was expecting an adverse reaction. I drop into soothing, almost apologetic tones. I save his feelings, then kick myself for doing so. 'I'm fine,' I say. In many ways this is what I want to believe. I can't afford to believe otherwise. Besides which, it is part the truth: I am standing and speaking; I am alive.

Suddenly, with a swift cruelty, he changes the subject. 'You need my money, don't you?' His question is a power bid; a client's attempt to assert power over a sex worker. By bringing dollars into the conversation he is attempting to put me in my place, or rather to discredit me to a place beneath him. I don't reply and when I do speak it's to ask him a question. 'What's the matter? What's all this about?'

Something clearly is a problem or we wouldn't be sitting here. We would be playing Josephine and Napoleon in Sardinia, Samson and Delilah in the Promised Land or Antony and Cleopatra at the Pyramids. We wouldn't be toying with white rolls and unsalted butter in an underground restaurant with no natural light in the middle of the day. I pick up my fork, and poke and prod at the cooling salmon steak that rests on a bed of slimy, sensuous, gentle leeks. He opens his mouth.

'There's more I need to do. There are demons I need to exorcize.'

'Meaning what?' I ask.

'Meaning that I'll come up with a script.'

We part, Luke heading northwards, me southwards, over the concrete of Martin's Square. I catch a bus and as soon as I get home I get into my car and drive. The last thing I feel like doing is sitting in my house, alone, all afternoon and evening.

I don't care where I'm heading. Motion makes me forget, or at best put feelings on hold. When I was a child, I used to spend whole afternoons on the Circle Line, going round and round the city.

All the time I'm driving I am being followed by the pale-blue Holden. I give the driver a good run for his money. I keep his feet pumping iron on the clutch for four hours on the trot. I go in circles, around the houses, taking lefts and rights at random. I turn on the radio, listen to some American R & B. Suddenly I feel twenty, free, as if the world is at my fingertips and ready for the taking. I wind down the windows, put on my shades, and try to head north. I cruise through suburbia, through the sleepy land of neatly mown front lawns and crisply trimmed hedges. I pass kids splashing in and out of sprinklers, and jumping in and out of inflatable paddling pools. I drive on and on and on, through one suburb after another.

It's early afternoon when I set out and it isn't until six p.m. that my belly tightens and cries out for food. I opt for fish again, twice in a day, to make me brainy, and pull up at a fish and chip shop. My legs wobble as I clamber out of the car and stand on firm ground.

A boy with cornflake orange hair serves me chips and fried cod in soggy batter.

'Want salt?'

The heat of the chips warms the newspaper. It smells sweet, like a cowshed.

'Yup . . . Where am I?'

He tips the salt on to the chips and starts wrapping up the lump of fish.

'Ugh . . . Sydney.'

'Where?'

'Bondi.'

I thought I was way up north. Looking out of the steamy shop window, suddenly the information that the boy is feeding me makes sense. I recognize my surroundings. Looking out of the window even more carefully, a second time, I notice that the pale-blue Holden has disappeared.

'Four fifty!' the boy says, snapping me out of my reverie.

I open my handbag. The front flops forward and about a dozen condoms scatter out over the floor. I give the boy his change and scrabble around picking up the rubbers.

'Can I help?' a man asks.

His voice sounds familiar. I tilt my face upwards and Dunne is peering down my cleavage. He bends over, handing me a rubber that has fallen by his feet.

'Fuck off!'

I grab the fish from the counter and dart to the car. Dunne holds his arms in the air. The boy behind the counter grins. 'Crazy woman, eh?' the lad is saying, and Dunne, in his cop's uniform, nods back, agreeing.

Later, to kill time, I go round to Anita's.

She opens the door and then scampers back into the kitchen. A chunk of Cheddar has stuck to the grill: the air is blue with a viscous smoke. I push and pull ineffectually at the grimy window until she tells me that it has never opened. I trip over a flap of lino and tip over Wayne's water-bowl. A wave slurps out over the floor. We leave a puddle on the ground and go through to the main room.

'What's up?' she asks, full of life.

'Everything . . . Nothing.'

'I have a session with Patrick this evening . . . Shall I kill him? Take it to the limit. Take him to the brink and then over? Shall I?'

'Yeah. Do that,' I reply. I am speaking half seriously, half flippantly. Her suggestion doesn't seem too crazy.

'How's the man?' she asks.

'So so.'

'Things OK?'

'No,' I reply flatly. 'Odd. They're odd.'

Luke is assuming dimensions, or proportions, that I thought I might avoid investing him with. 'I'm shit scared,' I confess, eyes watery, voice wobbling. Yesterday it was her turn to crumble like chalk; today it's mine.

She comes over, puts her arm round me and squeezes hard.

An hour later I leave, giving her time to prepare for her session with Dunne. On the road outside, a car alarm is screeching up and down the scale with an eee aw eee aw eee aw. A man rushes out of a nearby apartment block, wearing a white vest, bulging biceps, tattoos on them – a ship, the name Tracey, a red heart. He grabs hold of a brick that is lying in the gutter and begins to smash the windscreen of the screeching car.

A crowd of pedestrians – junkies, tourists, residents – gathers round him. The siren carries on, despite the fact that the car's windscreen lies in smithereens on the pavement and its bonnet now sports a huge dent in its middle.

I watch the man's fury for a few minutes. Then his bedlam is too much; it feels infectious and I need to escape. I turn on the car engine and pull out into William Street. As I do so a cop car draws up, its siren also whining. I catch a flash of the driver's face. He winks at me. It's Dunne, early for his session, now detoured *en route* by the pavement fiasco.

The car is hot, like a sealed sardine tin in an oven. I check in my back mirror. There have been times, like now, when I feel no one is tracking me. I said this to Anita, who thought they took it in turns to cover us and that probably another guy in another car is there and I simply don't recognize his vehicle. 'Like the stars, they never go away.' She said this in an attempt to pull me together in the hallway of her flat, just before I left. 'You can't see them but they'll be there.' By 'they' and 'them' she means our protectors, our guardian angels, the police. 'Maybe,' I say. We had swapped roles; she was the one doing the supporting, providing the positivity.

'We'll be OK,' she said, 'We always have been. We'll show them.'

'But how, Anita? Just how?'

We hugged one another.

Later that night, she phones.

'He's gone . . . I didn't kill him. Everything was normal. Just a bit of weedy beating. No blood extraction. Just a flimsy birch. Prick. He's pathetic. How are you?'

I do a raincheck. I had forgotten that she had threatened murder and her mention of it unleashes a lengthy fantasy in my head.

'I think I'm OK,' I say.

'Think?'

I spend what's left of the evening making lists. I have to manage myself. I scrawl out an elaborate shopping list and I put it into action later that evening in the local supermarket. When I get home I play Beethoven and I fry some Greek cheese, which I sprinkle with lemon juice and which I eat with beefsteak tomatoes, olive oil, and black olives soaked in garlic and lemon rind, and chewy Italian bread. I'm trying to care for myself, trying to be easy.

I make a second list: 'Possible employment'. This one remains a blank sheet of white paper like an unmarked gravestone. I am trapped in the age-old ex-hooker's dilemma: any straight job will involve prostituting myself for eight hours a day instead of just one. I need to find a job which starts at source and which will work from the beginning – something like gardening or painting dingy grey walls white.

Soon after I've completed the lists, there is a loud bash on the front door, then another bash. I grab the phone and frantically try and call Dunne, but the line is dead. Someone is kicking the door down and Dunne has gone away.

I tiptoe through to the hall. It will be a while before the door caves in; I have a bit of time to play with. I creep up to the peephole. The foot kicking the door with all the might he can muster belongs to John. Beside him, with a smirk on his face, fists clenched, spurring John on with every kick he socks into the door, is a cop who I don't recognize. 'Give it her!' he says. 'Go on. Harder! Harder!'

I freeze. I don't cry. I have passed beyond the point of being simply scared. I go into survival mode, which means that I act extremely logically without tears. The safest room is the bathroom where there are good locks on the door. I go into the kitchen, round up some tools of survival – a knife, a radio, some food – and then go into the bathroom. I curl up, knees to chin, against the wall.

The whole house vibrates. The kicks go on for five or ten minutes until, out of the blue, they suddenly stop.

'Open up, luv!' the stranger goes. 'Come on, cut the crap. I know you're in there. Open up. Put on the kettle.'

John snorts and chortles. There is a pause, then another crash at the door.

'Yeah. Open up, you little bitch. Do what the man says!'

Then he stops shouting and speaks very loudly. 'Jeez fucking Christ . . . We'll have to blast it down.'

'Save it, mate. Save it.'

Footsteps pad softly back down the path. The gate clicks open and shut. I suspect the pair of them are manufacturing another plan of attack. They'll leap over the hedge and come straight for the window. Ten minutes go by. I crouch in a corner of the bathroom, with my knees tucked up under my chin, hardly breathing, waiting for the next thing to happen. Twenty minutes go by, then thirty, an hour. Tentatively, I open the bathroom door and crawl into bed.

I lie rigid with my ears wide wide open. At dawn the phone rings. It must have been reconnected. I pick it up.

'I want to see you fall apart like overcooked chicken breasts.'

It is John's voice.

I slam down the receiver.

At eight, the line still up and running, I phone Dunne. He might be bent as a spring but he is still the best option there is. He gives me some cock and bull story about having been monitored all night.

'Dunne, I don't trust you.'

'I'll be round,' he says. 'We need to talk this through.'

Twenty minutes later a police siren whines to a halt outside my door. Dunne arrives holding two almond croissants. He hands me one.

'Breakfast. You need fattening up.'

'I don't want it.'

He starts on his, taking an easy bite through the soft flesh of the pastry. White sugar-powder flecks his chin.

'Where were you?' I ask.

'We were with you . . . You either believe it or you don't. You either trust or you don't. And that's your problem, lady, isn't it? That's your problem. Trust.'

I don't have an option about whether or not to trust. I'm on a receiving end. I need protection. Last night I didn't receive it. Dunne is mucking us about. No one is behind us.

'Your husband seems a nice guy,' he says, and rips off another chunk of croissant, speaking with a full mouth. 'I think I got him wrong.'

He walks over to the cassette deck, takes out some Hank Williams from his trousers pocket and puts it on.

'Got you, darling . . . Got you all stitched up.'

Hank's voice swoops and dives through the air.

'Know what I got from you meeting your husband in the park?'

'Nah,' I say, shaking my head, lost.

'A sense of my own misjudgement. Just how wrong I'd read him. He's a nice guy. I got him wrong.'

Suddenly I can't hold my venom back any longer. 'You puny, slithering little shit!' I hiss. The words slide out of my mouth easily, like shampoo on to wet hair.

He grins from ear to ear.

'Yes, I am. Yes, I really am.'

He crosses the room, moving over to where I'm standing. Very slowly he takes hold of my left arm, clenching his hand around my biceps, digging his fingers into my flesh.

'Tell me what you know about Charlotte.'

'Nothing.'

He pinches harder. This is it, I think; I'm going the way of Charlotte. He'll push me down on the sofa next and leave me for meat. He holds me very tight. A minute ticks by. I don't struggle. I close my eyes. Finally he relaxes his grip.

'Got it? Got the power balance?' he snarls. 'Got it?'

I don't reply.

'Understand who's on top?'

I'd be a fool to disagree. 'I understand. Now go,' I say.

He flings me aside and walks towards the door. The music winds to a halt, comes to the end of its tape.

'Enjoy Hank . . . A gift from a country hick to a town tart.'

And then he dances out. I watch him go from the window. He actually waltzes out of the front door and shimmies down the steps outside. He twists and he turns and he gives a heel-click here and a toe-tap there as if he is a man in love, as if Ginger Rogers is on his arm.

Luke comes round. He's had a hard day at work; he is knackered. He makes no mention of our last meeting and I don't either. 'Give me a soft touch,' he commands. Dunne is only gone half an hour or so. I need a soft touch too. I need all the soft touches I can get.

I tell him about my ordeal. I don't get a tender caress; I get a stony silence.

'I've been thinking up fantasies,' he says. 'Wanna hear them?'

Fantasies are the last thing I want to discuss.

'No,' I say, speaking my truth. 'Just when I need you you're not there,' I tell him. 'Just when things are as bad as they can be, you've gone away.'

'I know,' he replies, half smiling. 'But who's paying who?'

'Is this the start of it?' I ask.

'Start of what?'

'Of your cruel fantasy.'

'Maybe . . . Could be.'

That night he fucks me violently. He pumps all my breath out of me. I pant out a series of feeble, valid pleas: 'Go slow', 'Please be gentle', 'I feel fragile' and 'I've had a bad day.'

He takes no notice. If anything, after each request he thrusts in harder and more roughly the next time. As soon as he comes he gets up, goes into the bathroom and takes a shower.

He leaves immediately. Unusually he hands me a cheque rather than cash. The gold-embossed cheque, account at a snooty Melbourne bank, is double pay.

PART FOUR

21

A few days drip by. Luke has gone dumb as a plank and Dunne leaves me in peace. I lie on the sofa like a stiff with the shutters funereally closed. The most I do in three days is shit. I also sleep and I speak to Anita on the phone. We arrange to meet in a few days' time, at the Grill in the Cross. By that time the world might feel safe.

The only person who phones me is John. He sounds on an even keel. I don't allude to his nocturnal visit or to his cranky phone call. I remain neutral, like a thermometer lying on a table. If I heat up and let fear seep out of the cracks, one of the lead players, be it John or Dunne, will be getting the reaction he wants.

John calls to say that he is biking over the papers. Remarkably, what he says he will do he does do and they turn up, duly signed, two hours later.

He phones a second time, breaking into my silence like a shrill alarm clock piercing the quiet of night.

'They arrived?'

'Yes.'

'I'm off today.'

'Off?'

As in egg or holiday, I wonder, and then he says, 'Away.'

A friend of his, Mick, is going to New Zealand for a fortnight and has lent John his house in the country for the time that he is away. John will stay there for a week or so.

You'd have to be told about Frank's Grill. It is turn left up an alleyway, turn right down some smelly concrete steps into a cellar, and it is a hang-out at early tea-time, five thirty or so, for druggies, hookers and cabbies. It is run by a tall, gangly middle-aged man called, presumably, Frank. Frank knows, or makes out he knows, everyone's business. He's OK, but only just so.

The Grill is a large, cavernous room which looks part hospital canteen and part English seaside pub and which plays one single tape of Motown – *Diana Ross's Greatest Hits*. Plastic veneer walls give an oak-panelled English feel and pictures of ships and ship-wrecks hanging at skew-wiff angles lend a Cornish pub touch. The actual floor of the room has an altogether different feel to it. Its tables are regimented in neat lines and are made from ugly, yellowing Formica, and its chairs, perfectly arranged around the tables, are orange plastic shells, the type that socket into each other like Tupperware picnic mugs.

Anita is already there. She is sitting in the corner of the room, squashed up beside the wall. A newspaper is spread out in front of her, opened at the horoscopes page, fluttering under the over-head fan. She had called up earlier, sounding desperate. 'You are gonna show up, aren't you?' 'Sure,' I had said. 'You OK?' 'No,' she had said.

Frank's second-in-command, an even thinner version of Frank, comes over straight away. I don't bother with the menu; I order my usual – fried plaice, a wilting green salad and a plate of spongy white buttered bread. Anita orders a lamb chop, a large gravy and mushy peas.

'Not seen you in a while. Business good?' Frank asks.

In theory, he doesn't know what either of us does since neither of us has ever told him. In practice he knows what everyone does.

Anita fobs him off with an abrupt, 'Yeah, it's all fine,' and seeing that he is not going to get anything more out of us, he scrawls down our order and shuffles off into the kitchen.

Pretty much immediately a waitress carries a stainless-steel plate stacked with a pyramid of neatly arranged triangular slices of white bread and butter to our table. She dumps it and comes straight back a second time – this time with a jug of iced lemon barley water. Finally, after all this to-ing and fro-ing, arrivals and departures, we are left alone.

'OK, what's happened?' I ask.

Dunne (although she calls him Patrick) had booked himself into a session at four this afternoon. She had thought twice about doing it but had figured that she didn't really have an option. 'You *will* see me,' he had said, and he repeated 'will'. She had sniffed danger and felt that it was safer to put up no resistance. He would, after all, come anyway.

When he arrived he gave explicit instructions as to what he wanted. He wanted to be taken 'to the edge'. He wanted to be hung over death's cliff, and he said he wanted Anita to hold on to him by his feet so that he didn't slip over. The session would last approximately five hours – a marathon. 'I'm not on for that . . . I can't sustain it,' Anita had said, well aware of the psychological exhaustion which would be involved. Dunne hadn't listened. 'Do it,' he had ordered. 'Got it?'

She had balked at his request. Very few women went as far as he wanted her to go. She was scared of his demands. She was scared of making her stomach turn, scared of possibly being unable to distinguish, when she got to the cliff edge, what was life and what was death and where exactly each one's perimeter lay. She had hesitated and he handed her his loaded gun. 'I'm not paying you to listen to your qualms,' he said. 'Get on with it.' He rode straight over her. He wanted to be shot at, and narrowly missed. In many ways Anita is still Miss Innocent. She had never even handled a loaded gun. She told him so. She warned him of the dangers.

'That's cool.'

'It's not cool by me, Patrick . . . What the fuck happens if something goes wrong?'

'Like what?'

'Like I don't miss. Like I hit on target. Or off it.'

If that were the case, he said, she would be setting a legal precedent. He didn't care either way.

The session began. Everything was normal except that it was

accentuated; it crescendoed to a limit. The beatings started off as average whacks but then she was forced to inflict them harder and harder and harder, on and on and on until she had moved from flexible birch to inflexible cane and until she was whamming down a stiff rod with all her might on to his torso. The stiletto-shoe punctures over the flesh of his top back began as normal – average pressure, flirtatious pricks on his skin, no skin puncture, no blood extraction. But Dunne cried out for more, and again, as with the cane rod, she was forced to really dig her heels in, not to hold back. His back was soon purple and bruised and bleeding.

She didn't find inflicting such extreme punishment easy. Some-times a client might want the odd skin puncture, but not to be beaten up to this extent, not to be attacked with all her weaponry, as Patrick was asking her to do. Each time she cranked up the volume she would flinch inside and each time she would try to think of something else. But the point with this work was that, unlike straight sex, she couldn't switch off and fantasize. The session demanded her absolute attention. She couldn't wander off, float away in her imagination to calm loving waters, be some-where else. She absolutely had to be there, manipulating, prompting, giving her all.

Dunne swung from the ceiling, like a lump of meat, a carcass. His own movements had constricted the cuffs around his ankles and wrists extra tight so that his limbs were in the process of being strangled, their nerve endings and blood supply confused and working at sixes and sevens. She whirled and swung him round so that his stomach must have turned. He must have felt seasick. His face turned a rich, beetroot red but his eyes remained white and the eyeballs stuck out eerily, like the eyes of a trout on a plate. She felt his gaze undress her. She felt angry. She tried to welcome the anger, to use it to pull her through and take her to the end of the session.

An hour went by, then another. Even her usual acidic verbal abuse was wearing thin. She was running out of superlative insults. By the end of the third hour she felt bled dry, drained, absolutely exhausted. She was drawing on all her reserves of energy and imagination to keep going and she felt she couldn't carry on for much longer – not at the same pitch. She felt in danger of collapsing. And then he had demanded the gun.

At this point, I imagine she is going to tell me that she hit him. I imagine that Dunne is dead in a hospital morgue. I run through the consequences. I run through the next ten years in ten seconds.

The fact is that nothing went wrong with the gun. She had fired and had 'missed' and she had hit exactly where she wanted to: straight between two mirrors, into the soft plasterboard partitioning. She had brought the gun right up to his head and down to his dick and had shoved it into his arse, all exactly as requested. He had come immediately, making a peculiarly revolting gasping sound, something like the death throes of a huge, beached fish, a shark on the deck of a rich man's yacht just outside Sydney harbour.

The session was over. He looked stupid, arms dangling out in front of him, suspended from ceiling chains. Anita had gone into the bathroom and had put her head over the toilet basin. She had never been sick after a session before.

'Ever thought about it?' he had asked when she had come into the room, refreshed. He was still dangling from the ceiling. He hadn't asked for release so she hadn't offered it.

'What?' she had gone, hardly into the room with him, lost in her own world.

'Killing yourself.'

'No. Never. I have an insatiable lust for life, Patrick.'

'Seen your friend Ruby?'

She hadn't answered.

'I like your friend Ruby. Nice girl. Charming . . . You're all nice girls. All you lot. I'd like to get my hands on her. Squish her melon tits, tighten a grasp round that white neck of hers. Know what I mean, treasure?'

'Get the fuck out,' she had hissed, unchaining him. 'Session's over!'

He had clambered down and had pulled on his clothes. Anita started to tidy up the mess, putting away the dildoes and the whips and chains, opening the windows, trying to waft some fresh air through the room.

She had been bending over, picking a stocking up from the floor, when he had come up to her from behind and jammed the gun barrel into her. The intense pain had made her scream. He had pulled the gun out and had shot into the floor. She had turned, grabbed the gun from him, held it at him. 'Get the fuck out!'

He had obeyed. He had scurried out like a rabbit under fire.

That was last night. She had gone down to the Cross, had scored and it was now eighteen hours later. She was coming back into the world, seeing edges, and she felt very, very ill.

By now the Grill is filling up and there aren't enough tables to go round. A woman comes into the place on her own. She walks proudly, head held high, chest out, eyes scanning the faces and looking, it seems, for someone she knows. She is dressed in cheap lycra working clothes: a tight mauve mini-skirt, high-heeled shoes, and bangles stacked up her dusty brown arms. She is black, in her late twenties. She comes over and asks if we mind her sitting at our table. I say, 'No.'

Frank's man saunters over, calls her 'Luna', and takes her order.

'Trouble?' she asks me, referring to Anita, who is semi-crying. Her question is more supportive than intrusive. I smile back, with a conspiratorial, 'Yes!'

'I'm Sarah,' she says. Since the waiter knows her working name it follows that he probably knows her intimately.

I introduce us.

She gestures to Anita's paper. 'May I?' she asks.

'Go ahead.'

Her ringed fingers flick over the evening paper – through the TV listings, through the autumn pumpkin-soup recipes, until finally she hits on the news section. In the centre of the page are bold capitals: SECOND CALL GIRL FOUND STRANGLED. 'Read this?' she asks, and pushes the paper over to me so that I can read it properly.

The last victim was discovered at lunch-time today in her Double Bay apartment by her flat mate. She had died in the early hours of the morning. She worked for the same agency as Charlotte.

'D'you work for Elite?' Sarah asked me.

'Used to.'

Although Sarah isn't exactly dressed like an agency girl, she might be one. Barry likes to be able to ring the changes and prides himself on being able to offer a full, à la carte menu, with something to suit all tastes.

'D'you?' I ask.

'Yup.'

'Mind me asking,' she says, changing the subject, 'mind me asking what star sign you two are?'

'Scorpio and Scorpio.'

'I'm Gemini.'

'You're not put off by the attacks? Going to carry on working?' I ask.

She nods. 'Saving to go overseas . . .' She pauses, smiles, 'besides which, I have luck on my side.'

Anita perks up. She is a refreshing cynic when it comes to luck and destiny. 'How d'you know that?' she asks.

A psychic told Sarah that she was a lucky one, a special child, head haloed with golden fortune. She launches into a blow-by-blow précis of the crystal-ball session – an account which involves the usual formula of travel, extreme wealth and classy homes in the country. It is like listening to someone else's dreams: I feel as if I should be interested, but I'm not. Anita shuffles around, impatient. She gestures to her watch.

'Time to make a move,' I say, picking up Anita's cue.

Sarah is just beginning to relate a second and earlier psychic encounter.

'Yeah . . . Come on,' Anita goes. We stand up to leave. I wish Sarah all the best.

'You too,' she replies, taking a forkful of baked beans and, at this stage, speaking directly to me. She has picked up on Anita's cynicism and clearly believes that Anita is on the other side, operating on some spiritually defunct wavelength. 'See you again,' she quietly says to me.

Sarah died later that night. I heard it on the radio, on the news bulletin straight after Anita's show. We might have been the last people she spoke to; ours might have been the last conversation she had. She would have gone home to her apartment after having eaten, called up Barry, got a job and that was that.

We walk slowly back to Anita's. She is working at the radio station tonight and I stay with her until the taxi comes to take her to work. No one calls and her apartment is eerily silent. 'I'm scared shitless,' she keeps saying. 'I can't eat. I can't do anything.' She keeps repeating the line 'I'm scared shitless.' She says it over and over like a prayer. 'He can't do anything,' I keep telling her, knowing that I'm lying, knowing that we are pawns. 'We could run. Get out of the city for a few days, weeks,' she suggests, 'just get out of here. This fucking dust. This pollution.'

If Dunne really wants our blood and bodies, driving a car up towards Brisbane won't help us. Once we are over the border he would have an easier ride.

If we are the perfect pawns, so too is John. I put to Anita what I think is true: that Dunne found the perfect alibi in John and that all he has to do in order to keep his end covered is prove John guilty of crimes that he hasn't committed.

The next morning, John phones. He speaks perfectly calmly, without any pauses between words or sentences, as if he is reading a pre-written speech.

'The three nights alone in the bush have been one of the most intense experiences of my life. The house is an hour's walk away from the nearest dwelling and an hour and a half away from the road. Much of the time I reckon I am hallucinating. There is a presence in the house with me. I am aware of the sound of my heartbeat and simple sounds like the scratch of a pen's nib on paper.'

'John, are you OK? You sound pretty strange to me.

142

He puts down the phone without replying.

After Sarah, another girl, Tracey dies. Next, in a curious turn off-track, a couple of boys who worked the wall in Darlinghurst disappear. They are found later; both have been strangled.

Until now I have not put a name to him. Neither Anita nor I have. Although I am now sure who the killer is, to verbalize my thoughts has seemed too bold a move to make. Murder seems too great a crime to toy with, possibly to get things wrong over.

Now I put a name to him and call him Dunne. He is working fast. His life must consist of nothing more than killing, of going from one death to the next. He is guilty of five deaths in two days. It must leave him little time for anything else. I wonder if he eats, this man. I wonder if Dunne eats at all.

22

Luke comes round. He stomps in, shoves the typed-up 'script' in my face and tells me to get on with it. 'This is an exorcism,' he says. 'After this I will have opened up new channels for loving. After this we will live happily ever after.' He speaks earnestly. I'm not sure whether I detect a tone of wry cynicism or not. I don't think I do. I think his tone is shockingly free of self-mockery.

'Beat me. Beat me harder. Harder. Harder. Beat me. Beat me.'

The whip lashes down on my back. It doesn't hurt. It tingles. It makes me aware of my nerve endings. Then it whams down on the mattress beside me. It is a flexible whip – a piece of flimsy plastic curtain-railing which gives and bends easily. Luke has tied me up so that I am lying on my belly with my wrists and ankles bound to the four bed-knobs. I don't know when or on what spot the whip will hit next, whether it will hit me or the bed.

He called midday and said he wanted a session. He gave me specific instructions – read out the lurid, detailed scenario as if he was reading me a recipe. He said I had an option to refuse and that then he would go elsewhere. 'You've got friends. Your Sister Scourge has got a reputation. I could try her.'

Anita wouldn't do this stuff; it's the wrong way round, sub-missive not dominant. Still, just the thought that she might bend the rules was the match to my fire. It got me going. My jealousy levels rose like mercury to the top of a thermometer. 'No, I'll do it,' I had said. By this time I don't know which way is up or down. By this time I've lost my bearings. I'm like a goldfish: I'll snatch at any crumb thrown into my pool and hopefully I will spit it out later if I don't like it. Part of me will try anything. Who knows, if I enact this stuff as fantasy, then maybe what Anita and her mistress posse say will come true; I won't have to experience taking shit from any man, ever again, in real life. This fantasy enactment will clear my slate.

'I'll do it as long as there's a get-out clause,' I say. I know enough about B & D to demand ground rules.

'Sure. Of course there will be. Choose one. Choose a word.'

I rack my brain for one. I want to find a word which suggests sensuality rather than sexuality. I want to think of something delicious. I move to food and think of laughter. I think of slithers of sweet-smelling mango and dollops of vanilla ice-cream melting into his belly button.

'Mango. Whenever I shout mango you must stop. You must not go on.'

So that's how I come to be here, belly down, early evening, early autumn, Glebe, Sydney, Australia, windows open. The sheet sticks to my stomach like a black-plastic bin-bag liner.

He comes into the flat. He is dressed in a manner that speaks money. He kisses me gently, then he puts both his hands around my neck and he squeezes tight. I cough, then gag. I begin to struggle – kick, scream. I try to bite his wrist but my jaw can't reach down that far. 'Bastard!' I say. I stop bleating and he releases his grip.

He takes hold of my arms and pins them behind me and he pulls me through to the bedroom and throws me on the bed. Very quietly and systematically he puts my ankles into chains. 'Bastard!' I repeat. I say it suggestively, softly, as if I were calling him 'Darling'. With my free hands I undress him. He sees a packet of cigarettes lying on the bedside table. 'Can I have one?' I don't answer. He takes the last one. He smokes.

'I want you to kick the shit out of me,' I say. 'I order you to do that.'

He half smiles, half smirks. He doesn't reply but he kisses me gently on the lips and then slowly finishes his cigarette. After he has stubbed it out he takes my arms and puts them through the chains so that I am spreadeagled on the bed.

'You want me to kick the shit out, do you?'

145

'Yes.'

He brings a chair towards the bed and very slowly climbs up on the chair so that he is towering above me.

Then he begins to kick me. At first they are gentle touches with his toe, teases almost, then gentle swings, then he bends his leg at the knee until finally he boots it into me – kicking with all his strength, great relentless swipes.

'Say you fucking like it, stupid woman.'

'I fucking like it.'

'No, just say, "I like it." Leave the fucking to me.'

'I like it.'

'Tell me it's not hard enough.'

'It's not hard enough.'

'Say that you need to feel more pain. Say that you can never feel enough pain.'

'I never feel enough pain. There is never too much. Hurt me more!'

'For that you'll have to wait until later, bitch.'

I'm wet. I feel slippery between my legs. His cock is hard. I can't touch it. I can't touch myself either.

He stops kicking me. He is worn out – panting, out of breath with the exercise. He sinks on to the mattress beside me and sits down. I want to reach out, to touch him, to caress him. All I can do is lie passively, absolutely passively.

There's a candle by the bed. He brings it very close to my body, two inches away from my skin. He lights it and drips the hot wax over me – at first over my white breasts then down my stomach on to my thighs and finally between them. The wax hurts. It hurts far more than the whip or the kicks. There is a moment of exquisite pain when it hits my skin and burns and then the intense pain fades and it leaves a long stinging sensation. I squeal. I flinch. I twist. I can't take the pain any longer. I shout 'Mango!' He respects me. He stops.

He gets up, leaves the bed, goes to the bathroom. After ten minutes or so he reappears, fully dressed.

'I'm going now,' he says.

'Luke?'

He turns. He has his back to me so that I can't see his face.

'Just love me.'

I want him to take the chains off. I want to love him tenderly. I want to stroke him, to draw him into me lazily. He pauses. When he speaks back he does so very softly and very calmly.

'I'll be back.'

'When?' I feel like a child whose parent is going away for a long time, maybe for ever. 'When?' Everything I feel I am feeling at top volume.

He waits a while before answering. The delay is all part of the power game. 'Later,' he finally goes. 'All right?' I feel very very stupid, very very needy, as if I shouldn't want him to come back, as if I should be strong enough for it not to matter if he never returns.

The front door slams shut. Big tears trickle down my face and they run uncomfortably since I'm not able to brush my eyes with my hands or blow my nose. I ache. I cannot move.

I hear a rustling sound in the wardrobe opposite the bed. At first I suspect it's a mouse, or just a piece of clothing falling down. But then the cupboard door begins to very very slowly open. A man's leg pushes its way out. It stays there – just a single blue-jeaned leg – taunting me, frightening me, taking me to depths of fear that I have never yet experienced. It stays still for about three minutes.

Another foot comes out. I still can't see a body, only two legs. A voice follows. 'Hello!' It's John's voice. The whole of his body emerges. 'How are you?' he asks in cold mode, super super cold. I say nothing. I imagine I must look white as the sheet that I am lying on. 'Hello!' he repeats. Even the fact that he is dressed and I am not lends him a power over me.

I try to back into the mattress but I can't. I feel intensely cornered. I can't speak. I actually try to but my voice freezes and my mouth goes dry. Not a word comes out.

He stands at the end of the bed, straight as a grandfather clock. He stares and stares and drinks me in as if I were a glass of water.

He puts his hand in his pocket and he very slowly extracts the gun. He points it between my eyes. I see him line up to centre forehead. He fingers the trigger. Very very slowly he caresses the metal question mark. I manage a sound – a whimper. I snatch at the air in little gasps – twitches and bleats. He fingers the trigger some more. He lines up the gun, makes a big show of lining it up. Say it, John; say every God damn thing you want to say. Get it over with. I close my eyes. I can't stand to watch him any more. 'Open your eyes.' I open them. If this is it, then this is it and nothing I do will make any difference. His finger on the gun, stroking, stroking, is the only movement in the entire room.

'I'm going,' he finally says. 'I'll let you stew.'

The shutter doors swing open and bang to and fro in the wind. Outside the street is still. There are no cars coming and going and no chattering pedestrians. I can hear no squawking birds and no screeching Tom cats. I hear John's soft-soled shoes pad down or almost glide over the stone steps outside and then I hear the click of the wrought-iron gate opening and closing. And then I wet the bed.

In the hush of that moment, John fingering the trigger, seconds for him of prolonged ecstasy, he had everything he wanted. He had it all. Of course he didn't pull the trigger. The fact that I was paralysed with fear was enough. He had it then, this mystical it, in the cool space of his head. He wanted my fear, not my death. If he had killed me the game would have been over.

God knows how I manage it but I fall asleep. In fact it's not actual sleep; it's more like hallucinating on my own adrenalin, if that's medically possible.

I dream of John. He liked diving. He did a PADI course when he first arrived here, up in Queensland, on the Barrier Reef, along with the Poms, fresh off the plane. He was a good swimmer. I dream that he is swimming. Goggles on. A mask. A glug-glug sound of air bubbles. Water is his element. Night-diving is his speciality. He doesn't know which way is up or which way is down, when he is floating. His torch light goes out. I dream that his compass fails him. He is floating. I see him splayed out, arms out, legs out, adrift in a night-time sea, without a reference point, without the sun, the moon or the stars to guide the way.

I wake up with a start. The door is being kicked open and it sounds as if the Yale lock will burst and fly across the room.

'Get fucking ready!' a man's voice bellows out. Luke comes into the room.

'Mango. Mango. Mango.' My voice wavers. I sound feeble. I feel it.

It takes him just a few seconds to realize that something is severely wrong and to put down the fantasy. He doesn't have to be asked to unchain my feet and hands, and after he has done this, he holds me and rocks me like a child. I cry and cry and cry and cry.

'What is it honey? What is it? Sshhh . . . sshhh.'

I manage to tell him what has happened. 'John's been here,' I splutter out.

'Calm down, sugar.'

'I will be a new man,' he had said earlier, before the fantasy had begun. 'Honey. Honey. Honey,' he whispers, softly, gently.

That night I don't sleep at all. Luke manages to. He finally clambers into bed and nods off. I don't want to lie down yet. Nor do I want to leave the room where he is, so I get up and pull a chair to the end of the bed and I just sit still, and then I cry. I put my arms around myself and rock myself. I feel like a peeled hard-boiled egg. Just the light touch of a fingernail may damage me. At one point Luke wakes up. He sees me at the end of the bed. 'You OK there?' 'Mmm' I go, and he lets me get on with the crying and I respect him for that, for understanding something of the cleansing process. 'Wake me if you want me,' he says. I clamber into bed, lie on my back, take hold of his hand and squeeze it. He doesn't seem to mind seeing me like this – amoebic, without edges. John would have hated it; he hated to see me in any role other than strong woman. He couldn't bear his own imperfection, his own weakness, and any tears or insecurities in someone else seemed to him to be hideous character defects.

Luke is different. I manage to do something that I never

149

managed to do with John: I let go of consequences. This is me, I seem to be showing him – human, vulnerable, scarred. This all of me and you can do what you want, stay or go, and it's up to you.

Next morning at ten, Anita phones and she is gasping down the phone. For a moment I think Dunne must have his hands round her neck and these are her last words. She will be at gunpoint, he will be leaning over her shoulder, and she will be being granted her last request. 'Come quick. Please, come over quick.'

When I get there she opens the door and lurches, like a drunk, to the wall. I push past. She is in her work gear: a purple rubber dress, stockings, red shoes. Her face is truly awful: lipstick is smudged all over her chin and her eyes are dark grey wells, with trickling lines of tears and mascara running down in rivulets towards her chin. Her arms and legs are splattered with red. The blonde wig that she's wearing is also dotted with blood.

I push past into the living room. Crumpled up in a heap in the middle of the room, with a plant pot spilt over him, brown earth fallen over his body, lies Dunne. He is half naked. To be more precise, he's dressed in diapers.

In the background I can hear the shipping forecast from a radio in somebody else's flat and I can hear the sound of Anita throwing up in the bathroom. I don't feel sick. I feel nothing; in a state of shock, putting off the feelings. I go over to him and prod him. He doesn't respond. I go back to the bathroom, go in. She is kneeling, head over the chipped, enamel sink.

'Was it an accident?' I ask her.

She nods. They were in the middle of the session and the gun scenario had come up and she had thought how easy it would be, and somewhere between the thought and her pulling the trigger this had happened. Anita had dragged his body through to the living room and had tried to give him mouth-to-mouth resuscitation but he had died almost instantly. Then she had phoned me.

We go through to the bedroom, which looks like a scene from

hell: everything is everywhere and the floor and walls are spattered with blood. A mirror has fallen off the wall and lies in smithereens over the bed. We perch on the corner of the mattress, side by side like schoolgirls waiting for an exam in a school corridor. Neither of us speaks. The door bell rings and Wayne, locked in the kitchen, begins to bark.

'Cops. Open up!'

We go through to the hallway.

'Open it!' I say to Anita.

'How bloody come?' she asks. 'We haven't called them yet.'

I shrug my shoulders. 'Just open it.'

Every cell in my body freezes as she opens the door and John walks in. Wayne jumps up and John hits the dog between his eyes and grabs Anita by the neck, banging her head against the wall. I stay hidden. Then he grabs hold of her leg so that she loses her balance and topples over. I'm standing in an alcove of the hallway and I remain hidden.

Next he swipes at her face. She isn't shouting at all. The terror of his presence makes her lose her voice. The only noise there is is of her body crashing into the walls and of Wayne's barking.

Whilst he has his back to me I very quietly reach for the phone. Right now the priority is our own safety. In my waters I know that John didn't want to kill me but in the same waters I know that that is what he has in mind for Anita.

'This is what you get for fucking betraying me with that jerk of a cop!' he shouts as he hits her.

'Come on. Wait a bit! He was a client, you arsehole!' she splutters as and when she is able to.

The fight continues. 'I don't fucking care if he paid or not!' John yells.

I manage to dial triple zero, get through to the police and hurry out the address before John hears what I'm doing, or notices that I'm there. When he does see me his eyes pop out like pickled eggs.

'What the fuck are you doing here?'

He is so shocked that he momentarily loses grip of Anita.

Within the seconds that she has a free arm she grabs hold of a pair of handcuffs that must have been hidden under the sofa or something. John is now launching into me, oblivious of Anita. I let him do so, knowing that if I do there will be enough time between him being able to do any real harm to me and the time that it takes Anita to come up behind him and click a handcuff on his arm.

He whams his hand across my cheek. His other hand is behind him and he happens to be standing next to a wall with a pipe running down it. Anita grabs hold of his free arm, clicks the cuff on to it and clicks the other cuff to the pipe. He turns his attention back to her, and I grapple with the other arm. She points behind me. I hadn't seen it before but there's another handcuff there, hanging as a wall decoration. He's caught.

The police arrive two minutes later.

'You've done the job for us, girls,' is their first reaction as two of them stalk into the hallway and see a man handcuffed up to the pipes. 'Hang about,' the younger of the two goes. 'What's this blood, then?' He sees Anita's blonde and bloody wig lying on the floor, sees a trail of something wet running through the hallway from the bedroom to the living room. 'May I?' he asks, nodding towards the living-room door. 'Sure,' Anita goes. 'Come in.'

'Bloody 'ell!' is all that I can hear as she leads them into the room next door. 'Flipping bloody bloody hell.'

The other one goes through. There's a very long silence. 'It's the fuckin' boss, Pete.'

I stay in the hallway, glaring at John, who has been left suspended from the wall and who, with one arm out on either side, has inadvertently adopted a crucifixion pose.

PART FIVE

23

When I get back from the cop shop later that night, all I want is to be held. Luke isn't here. He has left a hurried note on the table-top saying, 'In Adelaide. Back tomorrow!' It's probably good he's not here; this is my stuff not his. In some ways it is easier to cope with it on my own.

I don't expect to sleep but I manage it, unexpectedly, with my clothes on, and I am woken up by the sound of his keys unlocking the door.

He greets me with a hymn to Australia. 'Oh, Australia is so raw, so beautiful, so empty!' he says. He took a spectacular dawn flight and the landscape below – red mountains, mile upon mile of uninhabited scrub, although he has seen it a hundred times before, is ringing in his blood. His hands grab my buttocks. 'Oh, Australia is so raw, so beautiful, so empty!'

In the middle of this the buzzer rings and I hear the ominous crackle of a police walkie-talkie from the other side of the door.

'Don't get it,' he says. 'Leave it!'

'I can't leave it. I have to get it,' I reply.

The young man the cops send mumbles through the trilogy of pronoun, noun and verb. He seems nervous and jumpy, new to the job of breaking big and bad news.

'Your husband died,' he says starkly.

John had walked out in front of a car. He had been released last night and had been put on bail awaiting trial. He had been taking a stroll round the block, probably trying to rest his hyper-active mind before sleeping. It was after midnight. A kid on the way home from a warehouse party had swung out of a side street without looking. The boy, a seventeen-year-old, had been changing a cassette at the time, switching on to Madonna's *Material Girl*, and his eyes weren't on the road, nor was his concentration. He was drunk when he hit John. John had died instantly.

I let the young man out and go back into the living room. I feel as if I've been punched hard in the stomach; I'm reeling. Luke calls through from the bedroom, 'You OK?' and I can't reply.

After a few moments, he comes through, bleary-eyed. He sees me sitting absolutely motionless, staring blankly ahead at the wall.

'What's up?' he asks anxiously.

Now, nothing more can happen. Nothing more can shock. I am empty.

24

Anita had admitted murder right away. As soon as the police had seen Dunne's lumpen body splodged out on the gritty carpet, she had turned to them and had said in point-blank language, 'I shot him. I pulled the trigger. Self-defence.' The cops weren't used to such straightforward talking; they expected female hysteria to accompany male death. 'Right, luv . . . ugh, right.' It had taken them a while to gather their thoughts together and to act naturally. Then they shunted her rudely, like livestock, into the back of a paddy wagon.

Four months slowly drag by. Her lawyer claims that she has a good chance of walking away free. Initially Anita catches the woman's infectious optimism but gradually, after the press become involved and begin to turn the pending trial into a circus, her positivity erodes slowly like limestone, and she begins to spout a rather more familiar line; 'In the whole of our history, the law's not been kind . . . Hookers are on the other side of it. We all know that. The outcome just depends on what the cops come up with.'

The inquest into John's death takes place a week after the accident. The young uni student has his licence taken away; that is that. I sit at the back of the schoolroom of a court in black. Nothing is asked of me, no allusion is made to what I suspect is the truth, which is that John had stepped out in front of the car semi-intentionally and that his death, like Dunne's earlier the same day, had been part accident and part self-willed. Death was both men's solution and natural conclusion. It was their way out. Neither full stop had been 100 per cent accident. I feel it in my waters.

I mourn for him. I weep and weep and weep. Up until the trial I drift in a dream state, part conscious, part sleeping, walking through the day like a ghost revisiting his ancestral home. The funeral comes and goes one hot afternoon, an anonymous cremation replete with piped music and wilting wreaths. I slink in last and sidle out first, avoiding the few eyes and faces that I recognize. Anita doesn't come; the press have caught up with her and she hadn't wanted to turn a private affair into a public spectacle.

The press have a field day with her. A slithery little journo phones her at the radio station and, within a day, a dozen or so journos, from all states, are on the line, recognizing a story that will sell papers. VICE SQUAD BOSS FOUND DEAD IN SISTER SCOURGE'S DUNGEON read the first spate of headlines. The next day the dogs are confident enough to link her radio therapist persona to her mistress status. TOP BONDAGE MISTRESS IS RADIO PHONE-IN THERAPIST. From then on the phone rings and rings and rings.

Anita plays it for all it is worth. Once the story breaks, there seems to be no point in holding back. 'I'll bleed the pack dry,' she says, playing one lucrative offer off against another, stacking up the grands in a bank account, buying a diamanté collar for Wayne and having a remote-control TV installed from the ceiling in her bedroom. As a child, if anyone stole her pencils or sweets, she poked and prodded them with sticks, would lead an assault campaign against them and then stick a note on their back, something like 'Kick My Arse!' She applies the same spunk to the press.

Ironically the radio station is supportive. Her ratings treble and her salary doubles. Night after night her voice breezes out over the city. The producer turns the issue into a moral exemplum. What someone does with their private life is their own business. 'We are here in the name of good, exciting radio.' Subtext: we are here in the name of good ratings.

Anita meets Luke for the first time just after the cremation. Both of them are waiting for me when I get home. She is squatting on the front steps and he is indoors, neither one realizing that the other is there. All three of us sit on the bed, arms wrapped round each other like orange peel.

Hardly any words are exchanged but by the end of the evening, when she leaves, it is as if they have known one another for years and the bond between them is all the stronger for the absence of speech.

Next day she calls.

'So I met him. *That* was the knight in shining armour?'

She pauses. 'Nice.'

He is one day nice, the next day nasty; not nice the whole way through but always edible.

'You given up working?' she asks another time when we meet for tea in the middle of town. We stay away from the Cross these days. Meeting there is too stressful; she is recognizable, people nudge each other and whisper. Here, no one knows who she is.

'I guess so. Yes,' I reply.

Luke picks up restaurant tags, pays for the car to be serviced and pays my rent. I am a kept woman. I have replaced one kind of working with another. I'm aware of what I've done and I'm aware of Anita's unspoken criticism. In her eyes any woman who lets any man pick up the bill is a closet hooker. Sitting here, talking to her, my new status fits awkwardly, like a slightly oversize jacket.

At night Luke's body curls round me like a question mark. Since the exorcism, or since his fantasy was enacted, our relationship is becoming more and more ordinary by the minute. He says we were washed clean and I choose to see it his way.

Now we can behave like an ordinary couple, whatever that might mean. We can eat scrambled eggs in bed, take walks along the beach, and begin to fall in love.

Some nights, with the candle burning beside the bedside, when I'm half here and half in another world, I have flashbacks. The flashbacks aren't dreams; they are brick-by-brick reconstructions of scenes. Sometimes the flashbacks are angry, disturbing recollections. Clients long since forgotten will loom up, spouting forth the usual insults – my lips are too thin, my tits are too big. Other times the memories are lukewarm or single images: a condom floats like a jellyfish in a toilet basin and won't be flushed away, a punter takes out his false teeth and leaves them in a glass beside the bed, another one sits in an armchair, watches me and sneers.

The flashbacks always occur when I'm with Luke. It is as if his safety allows me to feel them and to let them go.

25

A week before the trial big news breaks about Dunne. Until now it had looked as if John would be posthumously charged with the murder of Charlotte, Luna and the others. John was a dead man and an easy butt.

Dunne died without family or friends; the small estate that he had left needed seeing to. A slim phone book had been found squashed into the back pocket of his trousers, moulded to the shape of his buttocks by the weight of warm flesh. The only numbers inside it were work numbers. Finally when no one had come forward, his colleagues took it upon themselves to sort out his affairs. Detective Dave Dime had been dispatched to do the job. By now it is May, turning cold into winter, some three months after Dunne's death.

Dime had let himself into the Surry Hills flat which was only a few minutes' walk from the station. A few red reminders lay in the postbox and a thin veil of dust shrouded the spectacularly bare surfaces. Initially Dunne's flat looked as tidy and anonymous as the inside of his car had been.

Dime had turned round. On the wall behind him more of Dunne's personality was revealed. The entire wall was covered with a resplendent Country and Western collection. Above the shelves hung two posters. One was of a naked Dolly Parton. Her torso had been lopped off and someone had superimposed, via a collage, the naked anatomy of another woman. The other poster was of Tammy Wynette, stepping smiling out of her Winnebago. Like Dolly, Tammy was naked.

Dime had followed his nose through into the bedroom. A red, satin-sheeted, king-size four-poster dominated the room. The curtains were made of maroon fake leather. On top of the bed was a series of maps photocopied from a *Gregory's UBD*. Underneath one was a lurid-green plastic file: Dime poked his way inside.

Inside was a series of notes and photographs relating to each one of the murder victims. The notes weren't official post-murder notes; they were intimate sketches of personalities and tastes. The photographs were snapshots, each one taken of the girl, or boy, standing naked at an ironing board. The notes alone were evidence that Dunne was the killer.

Dime had referred his findings to the officer in charge. The next day all posthumous charges against John were dropped.

Dunne was guilty, end of story. The trial came and went and Anita pleaded guilty in self-defence. She was acquitted within a day.

PART SIX

26

By now we are out of the suburbs and are in the plain that lies before the mountains; a flat plate which is dotted with stud farms and racing horses put out to grass. The road becomes unusually three-laned. I press my foot down on the accelerator, as far as it will go, and we cruise noisily at 140 until the road begins to incline, and then, five minutes later, we are really climbing, twisting and looping in sharp zigzags up the side of the foothills. As we climb, any tension that exists between Luke and me seems to evaporate. I feel incredibly calm. I haven't had to work on this calmness, it happened of its own accord.

The main town in the mountains is Katoomba and the main tourist spot is probably the Three Sisters, three vast pinnacles of sandstone, named after aboriginal spirits, which stand just outside the town, rising out of the cliff-top like giant seventeenth-century sugar loaves. Once the initial ascent has been made from the plain to the mountains, the roads up here keep to the plateaux and, driving along them, most hugged by Sydney-siders' ugly weekend retreats, it's easy to forget that you are up in the mountains at all. It's not until you try and turn off the main roads, and end up down a dead end (there are still comparatively few roads built up here, few compared with European standards), that you realize the scale of the raw bush around you.

We drive straight to the Sisters, park the car, and walk to the cliff edge. Mile after mile of dark-green bush spreads out in front of us, uninterrupted by roads, train lines or human habitation. A coach pulls up and some tourists spill out, shake their legs, stretch and dawdle over to the edge so that they are lined up beside us. If we were in Britain, practically anywhere in Britain, their presence would be enormously intrusive, but here there's enough space to go round. I'm hardly aware of sharing the view with anyone. I feel quite insignificant, tiny, as if I were a small child, sitting inside one of Europe's vast cathedrals. Back in England, if it comes at all, the feeling of space comes in snatches. At the top of a mountain you can only look in one direction because if you look behind there'll be the lights of the nearest town or the twinkle of the farm in the next valley. Here the rolling hills stretch on for hundreds of miles.

I breathe in the smell of the eucalyptus and look down over the metal railings into the valley. Most of it is a dark, dark green, but every now and again, in the valley base, in the gulleys and creeks, there are small patches of lighter-green vegetation; patches of rain-forest ferns, huge cacti, giant spider plants.

We start our descent. Climbing down is hard work – like walking down a train track; the steps are at irregular intervals for a human gait. By the time we reach the bottom my legs are trembling, as if they might give way at any moment. We rest, sitting down on a huge boulder which seems ludicrously oversized, like a prop from a tour of Universal Film Studios. With the exception of the occasional squawk of a parrot or a red-tailed cockatoo, the sounds are muffled by the thick vegetation and the overall effect is of sitting in the silence and in the shadows. Every now and again an irregular patch of sunlight pokes its way through the latticework of leaves.

'I want to know what you do,' I ask.

No reply. He smiles cryptically. A leaf crackles as it is turned over by an insect. I leave my question, angry that he won't answer. I'll try again later.

We clamber down off the rock where we have been sitting and begin walking along the track in the direction of the ski lift-cum-train that takes passengers to the top of the mountain range, a few miles up from the Sisters, from where we left off. We walk slowly, saying very little, just taking in what is around us.

An hour later, we are standing on the platform waiting for the train to arrive when two teenage girls, mini-Kylies, kitted out in ribbons and lycra, come up to Luke. I've noticed them earlier – standing at the corner of the platform, nudging each other and whispering and then giggling, looking away, then bursting out in giggles again. The taller of the two, the slightly better-looking one, finally musters up the courage to come over. She holds out a paper bag and a biro and asks Luke for an autograph. He has been squatting down on the floor, with his eyes closed, and has missed all the preamble and her question makes him jump. 'Sure,' he says, and signs with difficulty as the biro won't take to the slippery, slightly waxy surface. The girl, Lucy, then goes back over to her friend, who repeats the performance, turning the paper bag on its back and asking Luke to sign on the other side. As he signs it she just gazes at him. The train trundles on to the ramp, a herd of tourists with cameras dangling off them gets out, and we climb in. The train is more like a buggy, a fun-fair train, open-aired, with a cage above our heads made out of iron rods and poles. Lucy and her friend sit in the seats behind us. I then notice that other people around us are also staring at Luke. They know something that I don't.

When we reach the top, after we have marched through the tacky tourist shops and are standing at the sculpture of the Three Sisters, I finally goad it out of him. He is not a pop star, or a politician. He is an actor and what he acts in is afternoon soap. His name is Gary and, along with chook, arvo and bottle shop, he is a household name in Australia. His contract is due to end in September, when his character will die and will be written out of the series.

27

Reader, I married him. I married the star of a soap opera in white! The bride – ex-prostitute, body the vessel for a thousand men – wore white! I wore a cream silk dress and I wore corny flowers like frangipani in my highlighted hair, which was curled, in innocent tumble-down locks, especially for the occasion.

The wedding took place in early summer. It was a Saturday morning in November and we hired an official and booked a priest and rented the amphitheatre in Centennial Park. The sun was shining hot but not too hot, and when the ceremony was over we moved from the stones of the theatre to the shade of the trees and, like true Ozzies, we had a barbi and roasted snags and drank champagne. It was a quiet affair – more his friends than mine – and afterwards we took a holiday in Guadeloupe and we lazed on an ivory-sanded beach.

And what of Anita? She too sailed on to calmer, safer waters. She made damn sure that when she walked from the court where she might have been pronounced murderess of Detective Sergeant Al Dunne, she used her celebrity status to her career advantage. She moved from being a small-scale radio airwaves princess to becoming a prime-time TV queen, and now her pillar-box-red smile shines forth of a Saturday night at nine p.m. and she dons her husky voice and stilettos and suit and puts marriages and relationships to right as sex therapist *par excellence*. Anita got where she wanted to be – a star in the front room of the nation, an accompaniment to popcorn and TV dinner. She's a big earner and a nice spender.

She gave up the dungeon. She took all that stuff to the limit, and once she had taken it as far as a human being can do, up to death, to its logical conclusion, she decided that enough was enough and she didn't need to do it any longer. She sold her gear, moved flat and that was that.

I lead a quiet life now. We bought a house and moved down the coast and the house looks out over the raw and billowing ocean. Behind us, cliffs hover and, on our left, a graveyard dug into a promontory juts out to sea. Reader, dreams come true when you marry the retired star of a soap opera.

Acknowledgements

I'd like to thank the following for their various kinds of help and support: Ingrid Anderson, Martin Bax, Eve, Jane, Sarah, Sonia, Carlie, Ronald Fischer, Mark Ford, Christine and Michael Frank, Johnny Lloyd, David Monaghan, Tony Moon, Rilka Oakley, Imogen Parker, Roberta Perkins, Marcella Roche and David Wallace.

Excerpts first published in *Ambit*, November 1990 and May 1991.